Freedom's Fire

By Elizabeth Sullivan Falk

Illustrated by Qi Wang

For my family, friends, and students,
who always knew I could.
—E. S. F.

To my family and friends, who give me strength
and support—the Johnsons, the Fraziers,
the Millers, and the Burks.
—Q. W.

Text copyright ©2007 by Elizabeth Sullivan Falk
Illustrations copyright ©2007 by Qi Wang
Maps copyright ©2007 by Tauranac Ltd.
under exclusive license to Mondo Publishing
All rights reserved.

For information contact:
Mondo Publishing
980 Avenue of the Americas
New York, NY 10018
Visit our website at www.mondopub.com

Printed in China

07 08 09 10 11 12 HC 9 8 7 6 5 4 3 2 1
07 08 09 10 11 12 PB   9 8 7 6 5 4 3 2 1

ISBN 1-59336-321-4 (HC)   ISBN 1-59336-322-2 (PBK)

Cover and book design by Jana Collins

Library of Congress Cataloging-in-Publication Data

Falk, Elizabeth Sullivan, 1950-
    Freedom's fire / by Elizabeth Sullivan Falk; illustrated by Qi Wang.
        p. cm.
    Summary: Four preteens from diverse backgrounds narrate the events leading up
to the Battle of Long Island, fought in August 1776 in Brooklyn, New York.
    ISBN 1-59336-321-4 (hc) – ISBN 1-59336-322-2 (pbk)
    1. Long Island, Battle of, New York, N.Y., 1776–Juvenile fiction. [1. Long
Island, Battle of, New York, N.Y., 1776–Fiction. 2. United States–History–
Revolution, 1775–1783–Campaigns–Fiction.] I. Wang, Qi, 1968- ill. II. Title.

PZ7.F193Fe2004
[Fic]–dc22

Freedom's Fire

By Elizabeth Sullivan Falk

Illustrated by Qi Wang

"Posterity! You will never know how much it cost the present Generation, to preserve your freedom! I hope you will make good Use of it. If you do not, I shall repent in Heaven that I ever took half the Pains to preserve it."

—John Adams, 1777

Contents

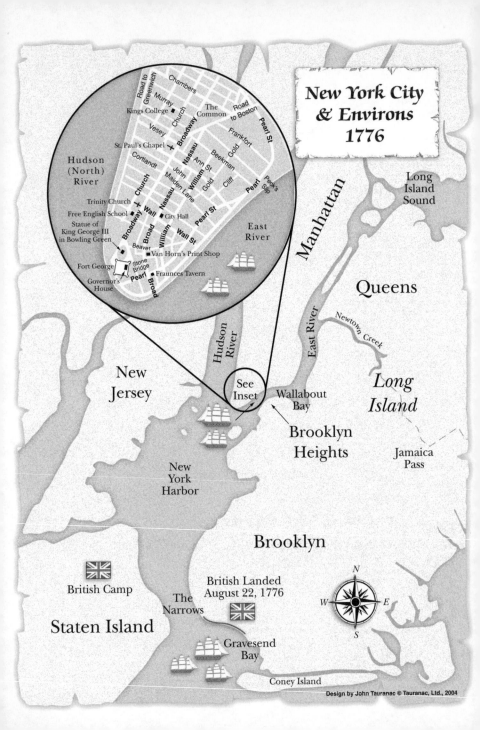

New York City & Environs 1776

Chambers
Road to Greenwich
Murray
Kings College
The Common
Road to Boston
Church
Vesey
Broadway
Frankfort
Pearl St.
Gold
St. Paul's Chapel
Nassau
Beekman
Cortlandt
Ann St.
Gold
Hudson (North) River
Church
John
William
Cliff
Maiden Lane
Gold
Pearl
Trinity Church
Wall
Nassau
Peck's Slip
Free English School
Broadway
Pearl St.
Statue of King George III in Bowling Green
Broad
City Hall
East River
William
Wall St.
Beaver
Van Horn's Print Shop
Fort George
Stone Bridge
Pearl
Fraunces Tavern
Governor's House
Broad

Manhattan

Long Island Sound

Queens

East River

Newtown Creek

Hudson River

See Inset

Wallabout Bay

New Jersey

Long Island

Brooklyn Heights

New York Harbor

Jamaica Pass

British Camp

British Landed August 22, 1776

Brooklyn

Staten Island

The Narrows

N W E S

Gravesend Bay

Coney Island

Design by John Tauranac © Tauranac, Ltd., 2004

Chapter 1
Maggie

Flamborough Head, England
April 1775

Maggie and her little brother, Sean, walked along a path edged with early spring flowers. The wind was frisky, kicking up the rocky chalk cliffs, blowing fragrant sea air under Maggie's long heavy cloak and across Sean's chapped face. They dipped their chins into their thick warm scarves and bent their heads toward the wind.

Wishing that she had minded her mother and taken her mitts, Maggie tightened her grasp on the heavy basket. It banged against her with each step, making her progress along the steep, narrow path even more difficult. She looked forward to the journey home, when the basket would be empty.

Maggie looked at Sean. She knew the smaller basket he carried was heavy for him, too. She called to him across the wind, "Sean, let's sing something. It will make the

baskets seem lighter." As they wound their way across the ridge, they sang:

> *Goody Bull and her daughter together fell out,*
> *Both squabbled and wrangled and made a great rout!*
> *But the cause of the quarrel remains to be told*
> *Then lend both your ears and a tale I'll unfold.*
> *Derry down, down. Hey derry down.*

They walked this same path each afternoon, carrying bread from their mother's oven to the officers' quarters just on the other side of the cliffs. As soon as they came within sight of the single-story brick house, they raced to be first to reach the wide oak doors—baskets of bread thumping against their legs with each step.

Maggie let Sean reach the door first and win the honor of lifting the heavy knocker to sound their arrival. Sean loved lifting the cold brass lion's head and clanging it hard against the brass plate. He struck the knocker once, twice, three times. They set their heavy baskets on the small front porch and waited for the door to open.

"I hope Daud answers," Maggie said. "I love it when he opens the door."

"I think he might still be away," said Sean.

"I hope not. I miss him so much," Maggie replied. "I hate it that he has to live here now with the other officers. I just wish he could come home and live with us again."

"He has to do what King George says," said Sean solemnly. "The officers are trying to make a plan about what to do with the Colonies. He would not be a good soldier if he didn't follow the king's orders."

"Yes, Sean, I know," Maggie said patiently. "I would not want Daud to disobey the king. But I still would like him to come home."

Just then the door swung open, and to their happy surprise, it was indeed their father who opened it. He stood towering above them in his fine red jacket. Looking straight ahead and in a very formal voice, he said, "Yes? Who's there? How very odd! There doesn't seem to be anyone here!"

Sean shrieked with laughter. "Daud, look down here! We're down here!"

Father looked down and said, "Ah, yes, I see you now." He saluted them and said, "Captain Cameron MacDuffie at your service. And who might you be?"

"Oh, Daud, stop teasing!" Maggie threw her arms around her father's waist and hugged him hard.

Captain MacDuffie looked at Sean with a confused expression and asked, "Who is this girl? Do you know her? And why, pray tell, is she hugging me?"

Sean giggled. "Daud, you know her. You know us!"

"Ah, that I do, son, that I do." With that, he scooped Sean up off the porch and gave Maggie a kiss on the cheek. "I see that you are being good helpers for your mother. The bread you have brought will be enjoyed by all of the officers here. How is your mother? Is she working too hard?"

"Ma sends her love to you. She was still waiting for the bread wagon when we left to bring these baskets. I don't think she is working too hard. She smiles and sings while she is working," said Maggie.

"Daud, when can you come home? Ma said I wasn't to ask you, but I miss you and I want you to come home," pleaded Sean.

Father set Sean down on the porch. "Come, let's get the bread inside." He lifted one of the baskets. Maggie brought the other. Together, they followed their father through the door, down a cold, dark hallway, and finally into the warm kitchen.

Maggie and Sean took off their heavy cloaks and hung them on pegs by the fireplace. By the time they were ready to leave, the heat from the fire would have warmed their cloaks. They would feel good against the chilling sea air. Captain MacDuffie set his basket on the long pine table in the middle of the room. He took the other basket from Maggie and set it there as well. Pulling a bench away from the table, he sat down and pulled Sean onto his lap. Hugging Maggie close to his side, he gave each of them another kiss.

"I have written a letter to your mother, and I want you to take it to her. It is difficult news that I must share with her. I believe she will find it upsetting, but I know that you will both be a comfort to her."

"What is it, Daud? What's wrong?" asked Maggie.

"King George is extremely angry about how some of the people who live in the Colonies are behaving," he answered.

"Why is he so angry?" Sean asked.

"Well, Sean, the king spent a lot of money to send our British soldiers to the Colonies to protect the people there during the Indian Wars. He expected the Colonists

to help pay for that war, so he wants them to pay taxes on some of the things we send to the Colonies."

"Many of the people who live in America don't want to pay the taxes," Maggie added. "They say they are too far away from England for the king to tell them what to do."

"Why will that news make Ma upset?" asked Sean. "She already knows there are problems in the Colonies. I have heard her talk about it with the other ladies."

"Oh, dear," Maggie murmured. "There is more in your letter, isn't there, Daud?"

"Yes, there is more. To be sure that the Colonists pay their taxes, King George and the Parliament have decided to send soldiers to America. New York City is located nearly in the center of the thirteen colonies. It has a large harbor leading into the Hudson River. The king believes that if our army can control New York City and that harbor and that river, then the Colonists will behave."

Touching the side of his father's face, Sean whispered, "You are going to leave us here in England and travel to America, aren't you, Daud?"

"Oh, no, Daud. You can't leave us!" cried Maggie. "It is hard enough that you have to live here in the officers' quarters. You can't go to America, you just can't!"

"Hush now, Maggie. Yes, you are right, Sean. I am being sent to America. I will go where my king sends me, and I will do my duty as a British soldier. And there is more. Your brothers Ethan and William have received their orders from the king and are being sent to America as well. That is the news that will lay heavy on your

mother's heart. You must do all that you can to help her. In times such as these, even the smallest person must be brave. Our country needs all of us now."

"I am sorry," said Maggie quietly. "I know I must be brave for my country. I will try, really I will. But I do not think that I can be brave just yet."

Captain MacDuffie smiled. He kept his arm around Maggie and held Sean on his lap for a long time. Finally he stood Sean gently on the floor. "Come," he said. "Help me with the teakettle. A good warm drink for each of you and then home to your mother."

As her father headed for the fireplace, Maggie looked at Sean. Slowly she reached out and took Sean's much smaller hand in hers. Failing to be brave for their country might become a secret they would share.

Taking a deep breath, Maggie turned to the cupboards and found three cups and saucers, while Sean brought the tea and strainer. By the time Captain MacDuffie had the water ready, Maggie had brought sugar and milk to the table. Father added a plate of molasses cookies. "The colonel's wife baked these," he said. "I snuck a few from the plate and hid them away for you. It is quite hard to hide food from these hungry soldiers, but I knew they wouldn't mind if I gave a few cookies to the fine young workers who bring them this delicious bread every day."

Maggie said, "Oh, thank you, Daud. We have not had cookies in such a long time. There just isn't time for Ma to make anything besides bread!"

Sean was too busy eating to thank his father, but one look at his happy face and Captain MacDuffie knew just

how grateful Sean was to have this special treat. As soon as the food had disappeared, he said, "Now I must get back to work, and you must go back home to help your mother. Remember to give her the letter. Your mother is very brave. She will not like my news, but I know that she will be able to handle this new challenge. Ask her to write back to me, and you may bring that letter when you bring tomorrow's baskets."

Sean and Maggie gave their father one last hug, retrieved their cloaks, and walked back down the dark hallway toward the front door. The empty baskets were easier to carry, but their father's sad news weighed them down even more than the full baskets had.

They left the officers' quarters and headed toward home. There were no songs on this walk. They did not even talk. Each was thinking of the huge ocean that lay between England and America. Several months ago a family who lived in their village had moved to America. Maggie had watched as the family sold their furniture and closed up their house. She had walked to the harbor and waved as her friends boarded a ship. She had walked slowly home, knowing she would probably never see that family again. Now it was her father and Ethan and William who would sail away from their harbor, away from England, away from their home.

Maggie and Sean arrived just as a worn old wagon pulled into their lane. The driver, a soldier named Terrie, saluted. He was always kind and often carried treats for them in his many pockets. On this day even the sight of the horse-drawn wagon did not bring a smile to either

face. Small treats could not keep worry away. Their pace was slow, and their feet dragged. Neither one wanted to hand the letter to Ma.

Terrie drove the battered wagon from the soldiers' camp to their house every day. It was then loaded with bread for the enlisted men. There were always more and more soldiers to feed. Each day new recruits arrived to swell the numbers of men already housed at the encampment. Ten other women in their village also baked and sent bread to the soldiers, but soon even that would not be enough to feed so many hungry men.

Each morning, after a small meal, Maggie helped knead the dough. The moist loaves were placed on the high rack above the oven, giving the dough warmth and time to rise. While they waited for the first batch to rise, Maggie and her mother made more dough. All morning they kneaded and moved trays of bread from the rack to the oven to the carry baskets. Maggie thought about bread all the time.

Sometimes she even dreamed about it. At the end of the day, when Maggie climbed the ladder to the sleeping loft and was finally able to lie down on her pallet, she sometimes dreamed of loaves with faces and arms and legs that chased her down the path by the sea. When Maggie cried out with her nightmares, her mother was often unable to hear—her bed was below Maggie's, back behind the kitchen. Maggie would come wide-awake after one of her scary dream chases and would need to sit up for several minutes to try to calm her racing heart.

Sometimes Sean, asleep on the pallet next to her, would hear her cries and give her a comforting pat.

Maggie didn't like to wake Sean. After all, she was four years older. At 11 years old, she thought that she should not be such a baby in front of her brother. At first she worried that he would make fun of her dreams, but somehow he knew to keep her nightmares a secret just between the two of them. This would be a year of secrets.

After the wagon was loaded and Terrie had left for the soldiers' camp, Ma said, "Come, you two. Let's sit down for a minute and you can tell me all the news." She led them back into the house where they sat in the small front parlor. Ma settled her skirts around her. "Well, how is your father? Was he there? Did you speak to him? Does he look well? Did you give him my love?"

Sean said, "Yes, Mother, we saw Daud. He answered the door, and we had tea, and he saved cookies for us. The colonel's wife made them. They were very good. We should have saved one for you, but we just ate them all up before we thought about how much you would have liked one, too." His small guilty face looked up at her.

"Oh, Sean, that's all right. I am glad that you had a treat. Both of you work so hard helping me. I don't know what I would do if I didn't have my two special helpers," said Ma. "But tell me, please, how is your father?"

"He is very well, Ma," Maggie said. "He was wearing his beautiful uniform, and he looked so handsome. When he answered the door, he pretended he couldn't see us. He even pretended he didn't know who I was!"

Ma smiled thoughtfully. "I do miss his smile. Did he send a message for me?"

"Yes, Ma, he did," Sean said. "He wrote you a letter." He looked hard at Maggie, who slowly took the letter from the pocket of her apron and handed it to her mother. Maggie couldn't bear to look at her.

"Oh, dear," said Ma. "From the look of you, this cannot be good news. Remember now, my loves, no matter what happens, we must all try to make the best of things."

Ma took the letter from Maggie. She turned her chair to catch more of the light from the fire. Slowly she unrolled the crisp parchment and began to read.

My Dearest Wife,

I am quite well and hope that this letter finds you in good health as well. I have recently seen both Ethan and William, and their spirits are good. They are both working hard in daylong drill sessions. You would be proud of their efforts. To have two sons follow me into a life in the military is surely more than a father could ask.

I do have news from the colonel. As you know, the Parliament has been discussing the Colonies for quite some time. King George has demanded that the Colonists pay taxes in order to help pay the debts that were created during the Indian Wars. This seems a fair request to me. After all, should

sending our soldiers to America to defend the Colonists against the Indians be free? Who should pay for it, if not the Colonists? Neither the king nor the Parliament can convince the leaders in the Colonies to comply and pay the taxes. Ah, what to do! The king says the Colonists are acting like misbehaved children.

The king believes that New York City must be controlled if we are to control the Colonies. We must display a show of strength and force if we are to get these rebellious Colonists to behave. Therefore, the king is sending thousands of soldiers to support this effort.

Yes, my dear, I must go to America. Our sons William and Ethan are to go as well. It will be the hardest thing for me to leave you and Maggie and Sean. But it will be just as hard for every other family who sends a father or a son to America. We must stay strong and believe that one day we shall all be reunited here in our home.

I look forward to your return letter. I send you my love.

> Your most devoted husband,
> Cameron

Ma folded the letter and placed it in her lap. She held the edge between two fingers and gently rubbed the parchment between them. The flickering firelight sent shadows jumping across her face. She closed her eyes and was still for such a long time that Maggie wondered if she had fallen asleep. She leaned forward and said very quietly, "Ma?"

Ma opened her eyes and rearranged her face into a smile. She tucked the letter into the pocket of her apron and rose from the chair. "Well, let's prepare our midday meal, shall we?"

"I will set the table," said Sean. He was glad to have a chore to do. He did not want to think about his father leaving. Sean had waited so long for his father and brothers to return to their home, and now it seemed it would never happen.

Maggie hugged her mother close, wishing that she could change the words in that letter. She had thought and thought all the way home about what she could do to change the colonel's mind. How could she keep her father home? But she knew it was hopeless. She could no more challenge the power of the king than she could turn away the tide that rolled in at the base of the cliffs.

Chapter 2

James

New York City
April 1775

James climbed down the ladder into the keeping room, following the smell of freshly baked corn bread. His mother stood near the open hearth, carefully turning the bread to bring all sides to a warm, golden brown.

"Good morning, James," she smiled. "Please see to your sister."

James crossed the small room to a wooden cradle. His baby sister, Hannah, lay on her back, waving her arms in the air and singing what James called her morning song. It wasn't really a song, but a long stretch of syllables that would keep filling the air until someone—usually James—lifted her out.

Just as soon as he picked her up, Hannah yelled, "Da-da!" This happened every morning, and it always made James smile. It didn't matter who picked Hannah up. She always said the same thing.

"No, I am not Da-da. I am James. Come on, say it, say James. You can do it! Say James for me."

"Da-da!" Hannah said.

"Your da-da is already busy in the print shop. He is a bit behind on the paper," said Mother. "Come now and eat your breakfast, James. Father will need your help this morning." She took a wooden trencher from the shelf near the hearth and placed it on the table next to a tall white pitcher. She put two generous helpings of warm corn bread on the trencher. James stood at the table and helped himself to a glass of cider from the pitcher. He took turns—a bite of corn bread for himself and then a bite for Hannah. He shared the cup of cider with her as well, being careful not to drip any on her long white frock. While he and Hannah ate their breakfast, his mother was already at work preparing the noonday meal.

After breakfast was finished, James pulled a doughnut-shaped pillow from under Hannah's cradle and slipped it over her head. He adjusted the straps over her shoulders and tugged at the pudding until it was comfortably situated around her waist.

"Oh, James," said his mother. "Thank you for remembering Hannah's pudding. She is so active now and wants to climb on everything! That will keep her safe from a few of today's bumps, I think. I don't know what I would do without your help."

"I like helping Hannah. Besides, maybe she will say my name sooner if I take care of her. Every day I think I will hear James, but every day all I hear is Da-da."

His mother laughed. "Yes, James, I know. She calls me Da-da, too. I think now you had better go to the shop and see Da-da himself, and leave Hannah to me."

"Yes, Mum," said James. He bent over and kissed Hannah's head and then walked to a door in the back wall of the keeping room. It was a small door, and he needed to duck to pass through the opening. Closing it firmly behind him, James greeted his father.

"Good morning, Da. You began very early this morning."

"Ah, good morning, James. Yes, I am worried about getting the paper out in time. There is so much to write about today." Mr. Van Horn stood in front of a large tray of letters, carefully setting a line of type.

"Did something happen?" asked James.

"Yes, James, something did happen. A postrider arrived early this morning with a letter from the Committee of Correspondence in Boston. It seems that General Gage, who is in charge of the British troops there, decided to march his men to a town called Concord to steal some ammunition that the Continental Army had stored there."

"But, Da, why would the British want to steal things that belonged to our army?" asked James.

"Many of the people who live here are mad at the British soldiers, and I am sure that the soldiers are just as upset. Remember that Patrick Henry stood up in the Virginia House of Burgesses and said, 'I know not what course others may take, but as for me, give me liberty or give me death.' Ever since, people have been thinking about the idea of independence and the possibility of war. When people who are on different sides of an issue

start to quarrel, sometimes words turn to violence, and people get hurt."

"What's an issue?" asked James.

"An issue is a topic that people may or may not agree on. For instance, if I tell you that you must go to bed right now, what do you think your mum would say?"

James laughed. "Bed? Now? She would say that it is too early for bed. She would say that I just got up and had my breakfast."

Father said, "Yes, she would. She would have a different opinion from mine. On the issue of bedtime, we would disagree."

"Oh, now I see what an issue is," said James. "What issue are the soldiers upset about?"

"It is not just the soldiers who are upset. Do you remember my telling you about the Boston Tea Party?"

"I remember that King George said that we have to pay tax on tea. He said that the money from the taxes would go back to England. Some men in Boston didn't like the idea, and they dressed up like men from the Mohawk Nation and got on the boats in Boston Harbor and split open the chests of tea and threw them into the water. The king has put taxes on lots of other things, too."

"Yes, James, he has. It cost him a lot of money to send British soldiers here to America to help in the war against the Indians. Now he is trying to pay back all of those debts, and he thinks we should help."

"Should we help pay, Da?"

"Some people think we should. But there were many men already living here who also fought in that war, so

there are other people who think that that should be enough payment. Do you remember the article I wrote about James Otis?"

"The man who gives a lot of speeches?"

"Yes, James, he is a lawyer and he lives in Virginia. He gave a long speech about how he felt about taxes. He said that taxation without representation is tyranny."

"Da, I don't think I understand all of those big words."

"Well, tyranny is when one person, in this case King George, gets to tell everyone else what to do. Everyone has to obey him, even if the rules he makes are not fair. When a tyrant runs a country, rich people get treated well, and poor people are treated horribly. Here in America, we have no tyrant. We have begun to think for ourselves. The men in each town get together and decide how the town will be run. Many of the people who left Europe were in search of freedom, and we are not about to surrender that freedom again."

James said, "So King George is a tyrant, and everyone who lives in England has to do what he says. What else?"

"I said we should not be taxed unless we have representation. That means that a government should not take money from people in the form of taxes unless the people who are paying get to help decide how the money will be spent. King George wants to collect taxes from us, but he will not allow us to help decide how to spend the money. Even more important is the fact that the money would leave America and be spent in England."

"You mean the king would take money from here and he would use it for things in England? That's not fair!"

"Many people agree with you, James. That is the issue that is stirring up a lot of trouble in the Colonies. Many people think that we might even end up having a war with England. I think that is what General Gage thought when he decided to steal the artillery in Concord. He thought there might be a battle, and he decided to take our guns before we could aim those guns at him."

"What happened, Da? Did General Gage get the guns?"

"No, son, he did not. Somehow a man named Paul Revere found out what the British were up to. He and a man named William Dawes put together a clever plan. They knew Gage's men would leave Boston either by walking along the road or by crossing Back Bay in whaleboats. They rode on ahead, but they had a friend wait behind to spy and find out which way the British would go. Their spy went to the tower of the Old North Church. In the steeple of the church, he was to put one lantern if the British were to walk out of Boston across Boston Neck, and two lanterns if the British were to go by sea across Back Bay. Mr. Revere and Mr. Dawes waited on the shore of the bay. When they finally saw two lanterns glowing in the steeple, they jumped on their horses and rode off through the night to tell the people near Lexington and Concord that the British were on the way. By the time the troops got to Lexington, there was a small group of Minutemen waiting for them, and an even bigger group waiting in Concord. The British had to turn

around and march back to Boston with Minutemen firing at them all the way."

"Will you put all of this in the paper so the people of New York City will know what happened in Boston?" asked James.

"Yes, James. I am writing about Concord and about the king's taxes today. I am reminding everyone about what the Huntington town fathers put in the declaration that they wrote last year. They said '...every freeman's property is absolutely his own, and no man has a right to take it from him without his consent...that therefore all taxes and duties imposed on His Majesty's subjects in the American Colonies by the authority of Parliament are wholly unconstitutional and a plain violation of the most essential rights of British subjects.'"

"Da, I don't want you to get in any trouble by writing about the British soldiers."

"Ah, James. As a newspaperman it is my duty to include in *Van Horn's Post* what people on both sides of an issue think. I always know what opinion I keep, but I must not show that in the paper. Now, perhaps, while I finish this article, you can begin to set the type for other news stories. Why don't you begin with the ship's lading? Be very careful to get all of the numbers right. I will check your work before we print, but it is much easier if I don't have to correct your errors."

"I'll be very careful, Da. Last time I only had two mistakes. Remember? Today I will try not to have any."

"That's my boy," said Mr. Van Horn. He reached out and ruffled James's hair before turning back to his work.

His hands were large and stained with ink from years of work in the print shop. Perched on the end of his nose were the wire-rimmed spectacles that helped him see the tiny blocks of type. His bibbed apron was streaked with ink, and by the end of the day, he usually had a trail or two of ink on his face as well.

James worked side by side with his father in the small print shop, both bent toward his work. The small room was crowded with storage shelves and worktables. James worked carefully to set the letters correctly. He listed each ship's name, its cargo, and its date of arrival and departure. Later they stopped just long enough to join Mum and Hannah for a noonday meal of bean porridge and sausage with tall mugs of beer and cider.

After their meal, Da got a large jug of ink that had been kept warm near the fire. If the ink got cold, it would get too thick to use. James set the first tray of letters into the massive wooden press. First, Da stirred the ink and then used leather pads to smear it across the face of the letters. He and James worked together to fit a piece of paper into a frame in the press. Da turned a large screw that pressed the paper and the inked type blocks together. In this way they printed half of the front page of the newspaper onto dozens of sheets of paper. After those sheets had dried and the second half of the page was set in type, Da and James printed the other half. The latest edition of *Van Horn's Post* began to appear, one page at a time. Only four pages long, the paper had three columns on each page. Along with the local and shipping news, it included a sermon, poetry, and a few

advertisements. As soon as the ink was dry, James collated the pages. When a stack of 20 papers had been completed, he lifted the bundle and headed for the door.

"Da, I'm off to deliver! Are there any letters today?" His father shook his head and James left the pressroom. In the front of the shop were shelves of books and several small boxes to hold letters. Mr. Van Horn not only published the paper but also ran a bookstore and managed the post office. James grabbed his hat from a peg by the door and rushed out into the street.

Early spring rains had left Broad Street a sea of mud. Deep ruts from wagon wheels made travel very difficult. James walked on long boards that had been placed in front of the stretch of shops. He passed the cobbler, a tinsmith, a cooper, and a blacksmith. He loved the different smells that came from each of the shops. Often, the man working in the shop would call a greeting as James passed by. Sometimes he would stop for just a minute to watch the blacksmith pound iron into shape, or to watch the cooper fit a band of metal around a barrel. But today he was too busy reading the article about the battles at Lexington and Concord to pay attention to any of the artisans.

James continued his walk along the rough boards until he reached Sam Fraunces' tavern. He opened the door and walked into a dark, smoky room. James swung the papers up onto the high counter and called out, "Mr. Fraunces, here are your papers!"

A tall, dark-skinned man came from the back room. He was busily drying a large kettle, but when he saw James, his face lit up with a huge smile.

"Welcome, Sir James! How are you this fine day?"

"I am well, sir, thank you. I have brought the newspapers for your customers."

"Thank you, James. Tell me, what news does the paper contain?"

Talking as fast as he could, James replied, "My da says there were battles between the Redcoats and the Patriots. General Gage marched a lot of soldiers to Concord to steal some of our guns, but Minutemen met them in the town of Lexington and tried to stop them. There weren't enough men though, and the British soldiers kept right on marching to Concord. Those soldiers thought they were going to just walk into Concord and take our guns without a problem. But Paul Revere, he's a silversmith who lives in Boston, he and this other man, Dawes, had ridden on ahead and warned everyone. They shouted, 'The Regulars are out! The Regulars are out!' So by the time the British soldiers got to Concord, lots of Patriots were there to meet them. The British fired, and right away they killed a soldier and a drummer named Abner Hosmer. So the Minutemen fired back, and the British were so surprised that they turned back toward Boston. All along the way, the Minutemen and the militia fired on the British soldiers. They fired from houses and from behind walls and trees. They sent those Redcoats running all the way back to Boston!" James stopped to take a breath.

Mr. Fraunces said, "Ah, James, you tell the news well. I would have liked to have been in Concord to see those Lobsterbacks turn and run for cover!"

"Me, too. Well, I had better get back to the shop to help Da with the paper. Goodbye, Mr. Fraunces."

"Goodbye, James. I look forward to next week's paper."

James left the tavern and hurried back to the shop. He had many more deliveries to make and very little time. If he delivered all of the papers with time to spare, his father would allow him to go to Bowling Green and read the news to the people gathered there. James loved reading to people who weren't able to read the news for themselves. It was his favorite part of the day.

As James made his way home along the boardwalk, two British soldiers walked toward him, deep in conversation. He had to step off the boards and into the mud to let them pass. James turned and watched the two men walk on down the street. One looked a little bit like his father. As the soldiers walked away, he wondered, "Will the fight for independence be fought right here in New York City? One day soon, will one of those soldiers try to shoot me?"

Chapter 3

Joe

Lord Underhill's Manor, Hudson River Valley, New York
April 1775

Jessie pushed the ornate food cart into the master's study to serve the family's afternoon tea. She had repeated this same chore every day for the many years she had lived in the slave quarters at Lord Underhill's manor. Usually she loved this room with its high walls lined with books she longed to be able to read. She never touched the books, but she often imagined what story might lie behind each cover. The heavy scent of brandy and tobacco in the room brought a small comfort to her busy days.

But today when she entered the room, the angry voice of her master robbed Jessie of any peace that might have been found there. Careful to make no noise, she went about setting out the silver teapot and spoons, the china cups, and the beautiful trays of frosted cakes. No one in the Underhill family ever acknowledged the presence of any slave, so the argument between father and son carried on as if no one else were in the room.

"I won't hear of it, Michael, do you understand? I won't have my son join that scraggly group of men they call a militia. The other riffraff up and down the Hudson River Valley can send their sons off to fight this foolish war with England, but not me. I will not see my son become a part of this rebellion. You will stay here with your family and continue to carry out your duties as son of a lord. There is work to be done, and I cannot manage without you."

Michael stood facing his father, the large gold buttons on his jacket reflecting the late afternoon light. "Father, you have an overseer who handles the slaves, a man who supervises the crops, several house slaves, and even more slaves in the barns and on the grounds. What can you possibly need me for?"

"Silence!" roared Lord Underhill. "Such insolence!"

"Careful, Father, your wig is wobbling. If you shout any louder, it is sure to fall off!"

Lord Underhill quickly adjusted his powdered wig. "You think this is a joke, Michael? I assure you it is not! You will stay here. Most of our profits come from shipping exports back home to England. Fighting England would be biting the hand that feeds us. Even if I agreed with these Patriots, these Sons of Liberty, I would never allow you to join the army. An Underhill does not serve; he sends a stand-in. I will choose a slave to go in your place, and the name Underhill will be represented in this silly argument. I wouldn't even bother sending a slave, as we can scarcely bear the loss of one slave's work. However, there are rumors that the Committee of Safety will be making sure that every able-bodied man of your

age runs off to war. Not my son! I will send a slave, and we will hear no more about joining the militia."

Lord Underhill turned toward the tea tray and took two cups of tea from Jessie. He handed one to his son, kept the other for himself, and sat in one of the large leather chairs near the window. Michael set his cup back down on the tray and stood in front of the large window, his back to his father. His long dark hair was pulled back and held in place with a thin strip of leather. He held his hands behind his back, his fists so tightly clenched that his knuckles turned white.

When Michael spoke again, he used a very quiet voice. "Father, please listen. This is very important to me. I know that you think we have no place in this battle. You still think of England as home. But I was born here in America and have lived every one of my 18 years here. I have never even seen England. I have never seen the magic of this monarch to whom you remain so loyal. King George sits three thousand miles away from us and demands that we send money. And for what? Yes, they sent troops to help us fight the Indians, but Americans fought right alongside the British troops. We are grateful for their help, but we do not owe them money. Any taxes that are collected should be used to help this new country, not sent home to a king that already has more than enough. If there is a war, I want to be a part of it. I want to help my country in any way that I can."

Lord Underhill's face darkened. When he spoke, his voice was thin and shaky. "Treason! My son speaks treason! No more! Not another word! You may have been

born here in America, but everything we own—every acre of land we tend, every ounce of food—came from our mother country, England. It is to her that we owe our allegiance. She made us wealthy, and we are indebted to her and to her alone. Michael, I warn you. If you persist in this matter, I will disown you. You will be no son of mine. You will inherit nothing."

Michael stared out of the window for a long time. His hands dropped to his sides. Slowly he raised his head and straightened his shoulders. "Father, I have no wish to be made separate from this family. I will do as you say. You will hear no more from me about the militia."

Lord Underhill said, "Well, at last you see the light. This is as it should be."

Jessie quietly left the room, closed the door behind her, and leaned against it. She breathed in and out slowly, trying to calm herself before she went back into the kitchen to face the others. She took a moment to straighten her apron and tuck a few stray wisps of hair back under her cap.

As she walked the length of the hallway, the faces in the many formal portraits hanging on the wall seemed to follow her every step. Some days Jessie talked to the pictures, telling them about her day. But this was not a day Jessie wanted to share with her painted friends. Opening the door at the end of the hallway, she stepped down into a small fenced area. Following a stone path, she walked through a fragrant herb garden, through another door, and into a steaming kitchen. Heat poured from the hearth where a large leg of lamb was slowly

turning on a spit. Two women leaned over the hearth, tending the food that would be served at the evening meal. Two young girls worked at a high table in the center of the room, kneading dough.

No sooner had she closed the door behind her than the tears began to roll down her cheeks. Shoulders shaking, she lifted her apron and held it to her face to smother her sobs.

"Jessie, you cryin'? What's wrong?" asked one of the women tending the fire.

"Oh, Clara! Master Underhill's goin' to send somebody to war. He's goin' to pick one of our boys to send in young Master Michael's place. Master Michael wants to go himself, but Master Underhill says no he won't. You know they'll send my boy Joe. You know they will. He's the biggest and the strongest. He's the one closest in years to Michael. And they know he can shoot a gun. They're goin' to take my boy!"

Old Clara and her daughter Camille stopped their chores and hurried toward Jessie. They caught hold of her arms just as she started to slip to the floor and helped her to a chair. Neither woman tried to disagree with Jessie. They knew that Master Underhill's word was law. If he chose Jessie's boy Joe to go, then Joe was going.

Jessie wiped her eyes and looked at her two friends. "Why do they send my boy? This isn't our fight! All those men say they don't want to pay any taxes to the king. That's all right for those folks. But we don't pay taxes. We don't have any money! This isn't our fight! They don't need my Joe! They can fight without him. They don't

need my Joe. If they don't want to pay taxes, then they need to be the ones that go do the fightin'. We do their cookin' and their cleanin' and their growin', and now we got to do their fightin'."

The two women looked at each other over Jessie's head. Clara kept one hand on Jessie's shoulder and held the other one out to her daughter. The women stood close to Jessie until her sobs began to quiet. The two young girls at the table watched the women but never once stopped kneading the dough.

The door to the kitchen burst open, and two strong men walked in, arms filled with firewood. They hollered greetings to the women and went directly to the hearth where they piled the logs. Busy unloading the wood, they did not notice that Jessie had been crying.

Jessie's husband, Ben, the taller of the two, laughed as he stacked the wood. "Well, ladies, you all are settin' down right here in the middle of the day. What's Master goin' to say about that? If he catches you, you are goin' to be some sorry!"

When no one answered him, Ben turned from the hearth to look at his wife. "Jessie, you cryin'? What did the master put in your path today?"

Jessie looked at her big strong man. She looked at her handsome young son. "Master is goin' to send our Joe to war," she said. "He says Michael can't go. He says he's pickin' someone to go in his spot. He's goin' to send our Joe, I know he is."

"How do you know this?"

"I heard Master in the study yellin' at young Michael. Michael says he wants to go. He says he loves America. Master says if he goes, he isn't his son anymore. Michael says all right. He says he won't go. They're goin' to send our boy, Ben. They're goin' to send our Joe."

"They can't send me, Mama," cried Joe. "I live here. I do good work for the master. He knows how hard I work for him. I work every day. He says lift, I lift. He says pull, I pull. He says pick, I pick. He needs me here, Mama. Besides, I haven't got but 10, 11 years now. No army wants a boy such as me."

"He's right. Joe's right. Master needs a big boy like this one right here at home," said Ben.

"My heart is talkin' to me now, and it's tellin' me that Joe is goin'; he's goin' to fight the master's war. He's big for his years, mighty big. No one is goin' to ask how old he is. They'll just take him. We won't be seein' our baby boy anymore," said Jessie.

Clara said, "Come on now, Jessie. We don't know what Master is goin' to do. But we've got to get this food done. Food not done for supper, somebody will be hurtin'. Stand up, Jessie, and help me get the cookin' done. Then we'll see about your boy."

Jessie closed her eyes. She reached up to pat Clara's hand that still lay on her shoulder. Her huge sigh filled the room. No one moved. The young kitchen girls stopped working, their hands still on the dough. Ben crossed the room and knelt at Jessie's feet.

"Jessie girl, we got to go on now. We got to get the work done. We'll hear soon from the master. Joe's here now. He's right here. Him and me, we're goin' to go back out now. We've got work mendin' them fences. Get up, girl. Joe's still here now."

Jessie opened her eyes and took her husband's hands in her own. For a long moment, they looked into each other eyes, and then slowly Jessie stood. She dropped Ben's hands. Walking toward the hearth, she touched Joe's cheek as she passed him.

Joe smiled at his mother. "Mama, you save me some of that lamb. You carve it up, you put some in your pocket, hear? My mouth is goin' to be thinkin' about that lamb till I see you later. Papa is goin' to be wantin' some, too."

Jessie said, "I'll save it for you both. Go on now; get out of my kitchen."

Ben and Joe left, closing the door behind them. Clara and Camille joined Jessie at the hearth. Each woman tended a different pot. The girls patted the dough into round loaves and put them on a wooden tray. One of the girls covered the tray with a cloth and carried it over to a high shelf near the hearth.

As she stirred a pot full of turnips, tears still ran down Jessie's face. She began to hum a slow, mournful song. Clara joined in the humming. The women did not look at each other, and they did not speak. Camille began to sing. Her low, rich voice filled the kitchen, giving song to their sadness.

You got a right, I got a right,
We all got a right to the tree of life;
Yes, you got a right, I got a right,
We all got a right to the tree of life.
The very time I thought I was los'
The dungeon shook an' the chain fell off.
You may hinder me here
But you cannot there
'Cause God in his heaven
Goin' to answer prayer.
O Brethren, you got a right,
I got a right,
We all got a right to the tree of life.

One of the girls left the kitchen to pick some herbs from the garden. In passing she told another slave what had happened in the master's study. Slowly the news that Joe might be sent to war for Michael made its way in whispers to the many slaves who worked at Underhill Manor. Each man and woman reacted with the same sadness and fear. Hoes moved faster, and axes swung harder as anger worked its way from hearts and minds to arms and hands. One of the heaviest chains of slavery was this feeling of helplessness; Joe would be sent away, and nothing could stop it.

Someone in the cornfield began to sing. Others joined in. Songs about courage and hope wound their way from the apple orchard and the planting fields to Jessie's kitchen, filling her heart. The music found Joe and Ben at work in the barns and wrapped around them. Neither

Ben nor his son stopped working, but they began to move their bodies in time to the hymns. Joe opened his heart to the songs and tucked away the words and music for a time to come, when he knew he would need to hear them again.

Jessie, Clara, and Camille served the evening meal of roasted lamb and garden vegetables to Lord Underhill and his family in the large formal dining room. Mrs. Underhill and the three Underhill daughters wore beautiful brocade gowns, each a different pastel color. They spent the meal talking and laughing about the latest fashions in hats, and Lord Underhill's and Michael's unusual silence went unnoticed. Only Jessie noticed, and their silence confirmed what she already feared. She had hoped that Lord Underhill would change his mind and allow Michael to join the army and fight for his country. But now she knew that had not happened. No such peace had been made, and this father and son were still angry with each other.

After the family left the dining room, the house slaves worked quietly to clear all of the dishes and food from the table. Back in the kitchen, plates and pans were washed and food was stored. When everything had been made tidy in anticipation of the morning meal, Jessie left the kitchen with the other women and walked back to the small shacks behind the barns.

Clara, Jessie, and Camille entered one of the shacks to find that Ben had already built up the small fire. The spring evening air was cool, and the heat from the fire was a fine welcome home. The small room held a few

benches, sleeping pallets, and a spinning wheel. Some simple tools and one iron pot hung from hooks on the wall. The overseer always made sure there was a good supply of candles in the shack so that the women could work on the spinning wheel far into the night.

Clara sat down on one of the low benches next to a thin gray-haired man. "How's my husband tonight?"

"I'm fine, girl, I'm fine. We were out workin' the dirt, turnin' it over all day today. My feet are glad to be home." He patted Clara's knee and left his hand on her leg. She rested her head on his shoulder.

Jessie sat on another rough bench next to Ben. He immediately took her hand in his, and the two sat without saying a word.

Clara whispered, "If that overseer Jack comes here, that will be the sign that Joe is goin'."

"You hush now, girl," said Ben. "There's no one comin'. Joe will be just fine."

"I hope you're...." But before Jessie could finish her thought, the door of the shack banged open, and a tall figure filled the void. "Ben, send out your boy. We got business," he snarled.

Ben stood and walked over to the door. "Evenin', Master Jack," he said politely. "We're just about to have our supper. Want to join in? We got plenty."

"I don't want any of your slop. You hear me? Send out the boy. Best be saying your goodbyes; he won't be coming back. Don't fight me, Ben. There are more men here behind me, and each one of them is carrying a

weapon. You can send out your boy, or you can lose your whole family. What'll it be, Ben?"

Before his father could answer, Joe stood up and walked toward his mother. He knelt at her feet and put his head in her lap. She gently smoothed his hair and then slowly lifted his face up to meet hers. She kissed him on each cheek, held him hard, and said, "You always walk tall, Joe. You carry all of us right here in your heart." She touched his chest and then once more held his face in her hands.

The overseer pushed Ben back, took two large steps to reach Joe, and grabbed him by the arm. "Let's go, move it, boy." He pulled Joe out of the cabin. Ben reached for him as he was pulled past, and he, too, gently touched the boy's face. The door slammed, and Joe was gone.

No one in the shack spoke. There were no tears. Jessie slipped from the bench and crumpled onto the floor. Ben stood by the door, his hand still raised to touch his son's face. Wind whistled through the cracks in the walls, sending lonely sparks flying toward the ceiling.

Chapter 4

Taipa

Lower Hudson River Valley, New York
April 1775

Taipa (She-Spreads-Her-Wings) had just finished helping her family move their belongings from their winter fort to their summer wigwam. The winter had been long and hard, with many heavy snowfalls. She was glad to feel the sun's warmth once again and to hear the water moving freely in the great Mahicanituk. This season of renewal brought her great happiness. With time the lonesome winter branches of the trees would be covered with budding leaves, and the riverbank would be home for wild flowers and sweet grass.

Grandfather walked over and sat next to her on the short hard bench in front of their wigwam. Without speaking he took his knife from its sheath and began to whittle a piece of wood.

"Nixkamich (Grandfather), tell me about the ones who came before," said Taipa.

"Ah, that is a story you have asked for many times, and one that I, too, enjoy. It is the story of your ancestors.

Once long ago, when the river teemed with fish and the land was honored and respected, many of our people lived here. Before the white men came to steal our land, to set and betray treaties, our nation, the Wappingers, cared for this land. If you walked the trail on this side of the river, you would find 25 or 30 villages of our people. There were so many of us, it would have taken you a day just to get a good count.

"You would have been welcome in each of those villages. Men hunted in the forests and on the rivers. Women planted corn and beans and squash. Life was good. The Great Spirit smiled on the Wappingers because we took care of Mother Earth. Seasons came and went, and nature provided for us all."

"Then what happened, Nixkamich?"

"One day a group of men were at the river. They saw something floating on the water. Something huge. As it came closer, they guessed that it was a large house. Soon they were able to see men in fancy clothes standing on the floor of this house. Before our people could even raise a hand in greeting, shots were fired, and musket balls rained down. They had never heard a gunshot before; they did not understand the danger they were in. Two of our men lay dead."

"But it was not a house floating on the water," prompted Taipa.

"No, it was not. It was a ship that had sailed across the big water. The men on the ship were exploring new lands, and they had orders from their rulers to take any land they found. They even kidnapped some of our

people and took them back to their homeland to work as slaves. More and more ships came."

"Were all of the people on the ships bad people?"

"No. Some were good. Henry Hudson came in one of the large ships. White people now call this river the Hudson. He was a kind man who wanted to know all about this land. He wanted to trade things he had brought with him for beaver skins. The skins would be taken back to his homeland to be made into fancy hats for rich men."

"I think those rich men should have done their own hunting."

"They could have, if they had put their minds to it. Sometimes people who have money don't try to do things for themselves. They pay other people to do it for them."

"Did the people trust the explorers?" asked Taipa.

"I think that there could have been trust. But the people always remembered the men who were killed and the men and women who were kidnapped. No explorer was completely trusted. The people were very watchful of the men who came to trade."

"What happened to all of our people? If there were 30 villages here, where did all of those people go? There are less than 100 of us left!"

"The Wappingers had lived here in harmony and balance with nature, but many dangers came with the ships. The white men brought things with them that the people had never seen before. Soon we did not make our clay pots anymore; we traded animal skins for iron pots. We had always hunted for the food we needed with bow

and arrow. Once the men of the Wappingers saw how clever the musket was, we traded skins for muskets. Soon the forest was full of the sound of musket fire.

The white men also brought alcohol. Our people had never tasted this firewater called rum. They did not know it would be poison for their souls. Some of the people who drank the rum soon wanted more and more of it. They ignored their chores and their families, and were only interested in rum."

"Rum and musket balls couldn't have taken away so many hundreds of people, could they, Nixkamich?"

"They took many, but the worst was the smallpox and the malaria. These diseases our people had never known came over on the white man's ships. Our people traded for heavy wool blankets. Winters are cold and the blankets were good warmth against the strong winds. The blankets carried smallpox to our people. Hundreds of people became sick. We had no medicine for it. Our herbs did not work, and our medicine men could not help. Slowly the pox and the malaria killed off hundreds more of our people."

"So that is why there are so few of us living here today."

"That is why. After the battles and the diseases had killed so many, most of the remaining Wappinger people decided to move west to be away from this danger. I did not want to leave this beautiful land and this mighty river. I convinced your grandmother and a few other families to stay even in the face of such great danger. Now your grandmother calls me the stubborn one."

Nixkamich had been whittling as he answered Taipa's questions. The piece of wood had taken on the shape of a small, delicate bird. He handed it to his granddaughter. "This is for you. Come now, we must help your mother turn over the soil."

Taipa giggled. "You want to work with the women?"

"The work the women do is very important. We could not live without the food they harvest. I have had many years of hunting and being a warrior. These old hands and this old heart enjoy working the earth. Farmers are honorable people."

Taipa took Nixkamich's hand. Together the two walked away from their wigwam. They walked past a large long house in which all of the meetings and celebrations were held. They passed several other wigwams and continued on through the doorway of a fence that enclosed their village, to the fields just beyond.

Across the span of one large field, a line of women and girls walked forward, each armed with a short hoe. Drawing the iron part of the hoe through the soil, the women turned over large clumps of dirt. The soil needed to be prepared to receive the seeds.

When the sun and the air had been worked into the dirt, the women would plant corn seeds. Four seeds would be placed in hillocks two or three large steps apart. Later on they would plant first beans and then squash around each little hill. The beanstalks would wind up and around the stalks of corn. The large leaves of the squash would shade the soil and would discourage weeds. Other fields would be planted with tobacco seeds.

Taipa's mother turned from her work to greet them. "Hello, daughter. Hello, Father. Come and join our line. The earth is glad today that we are stirring it up. It is glad to feel the warmth of Grandmother Sun."

"Hello, Mother. Look at the bird that Nixkamich has carved for me! I will make a string for it and wear it around my neck."

"That is a beautiful bird. You are lucky to have such a clever grandfather."

Grandfather and Taipa joined the line of workers as it advanced across the field, helping to bring the soil to life for another season. All through the day, the people worked the field, breaking it apart to let in the warm spring air. When they reached the end of the hillocks, shadows had begun to stretch across the field. The matron in charge of planting said, "Thank you for working so hard on this day. We will stop now. When the sun rises, we will begin again."

The women shouldered their hoes and walked in twos and threes back toward the village. Laughter and words flew back and forth between the groups as they made their way home to their wigwams.

A small boy ran up to the women and said, "Everyone must come to the long house. There will be a meeting."

"What is the news? What is wrong?" one woman asked.

The young boy did not answer. He ran on out to other fields to announce the meeting to the workers there.

Taipa took the hoes from Mother and Grandfather. She ran on ahead so that she would have time to hang the hoes in their wigwam before the meeting began. As she

ran, she saw a flock of geese flying overhead, winging their way back home from warmer lands. Taipa smiled at this sign of the new season.

When she reached the long house, people were seated on benches all around the perimeter of the room. She sat on the floor at her mother's feet. As soon as the people had settled in and the talking had stopped, a tall man stood and walked to the center of the room.

Taipa leaned back on her mother's legs and asked, "What will Askuwheteau (He-Who-Keeps-Watch) tell us? Is it trouble?" But her mother only shook her head and motioned for her to be still.

Askuwheteau said, "Thank you for coming to this house to hear these words. We thank the Great Spirit for looking after us. We are thankful for the new season of rebirth, and we give thanks for the fertile fields and thriving forests that surround us. We give thanks for Grandmother Sun who sends her light and warmth to waken the fields, long asleep during the seasons of snow. We ask the Great Spirit for guidance as we face a difficult time.

"We have watched as the white men and women who have come to live near the great river begin to fight with each other. We have listened to our elders, who tell of a time of great peace before these white people came to this land. They fight now over money. They are brothers and sisters, and they cannot find a way to share that is agreeable to both sides. The English brothers expect to take some money from the white men who live here. The American brothers do not want to give this money. The English ask

us to stand on their side. The Americans ask us to stand on their side.

"When we were first asked this question, we decided that we would not take sides. We answered that we would live here as we always have. We told the Americans and the English that we would live next to the battle but not be a part of it. The elders fear that now that answer is not enough. There is fear that the battle will come here to our home, and that if we do not choose a side, we will lose our home. Many of us have died or been forced to move to other lands. The elders fear that the few of us who are left will soon be pushed from our home here on the Great River. I ask all of you now to think of this question and tell me what is in your hearts."

The people were very quiet. Even the youngest knew not to speak. Finally Nixkamich stood. He said, "These men were once brothers. They all once lived in the land across the big water. Now they argue over money. They have forgotten their ties to each other. They have allowed money to come between them. This is a lesson for all of us here today to never allow money matters to come between brothers and sisters."

"What will happen if we choose a side?" asked a young woman who held a small baby in her lap. "Will we be expected to carry weapons and fight?"

"If war comes and we have declared loyalty to one side, we will join them in defending the land," Askuwheteau replied. The question today is do we remain neutral or do we choose a side? If we choose a side, which side will we take?"

"It takes no courage to remain neutral," said a man leaning against the wall by the door. "That is for children and cowards." His face was dark with anger, and his words were loud and harsh.

Nixkamich answered before Askuwheteau could. "I am an old man who has seen many seasons and learned many things. One thing I know to be true is that it takes more courage to remain neutral than it does to fight. That is why we must be clear on the reasons behind the battle before we decide what our people will do."

The angry man did not speak, but he turned his face away from Nixkamich.

Taipa's mother spoke. "We have remained neutral for many moons. This is not the first time we have been asked to choose sides. Each time we take skins to trade at the fort in New York City, we see more guns and more soldiers. There are ships now in the water around the city. These are British ships with big guns. We can stand here and say we will not fight, but that will not stop the cannonballs and musket balls from flying into our village. The white men have told us that they will not take our lands, but we cannot trust them. There have been too many lies, too many betrayals. We must choose."

"If we side with the British and lose, the British soldiers will go home to England. What will become of us then?" asked Askuwheteau. "Americans, angry with us for siding with the British, will surround us. If we side with the Americans and lose the battle, we can leave here and travel to our brothers of the Oneida Nation in the West. If we stay neutral, then both sides may fire on us."

Many people took turns speaking. The arguments seemed to go round and round for a very long time. Taipa lost track of how many people stood to share their words with the others.

When very little light was left, Askuwheteau once again stood in the center of the room. "I have listened with an open mind to all of the speakers," he said. "Now we must come together in a decision that will be supported by all of us. I will travel to New York City tomorrow. I will tell the Americans that we will stand with them. Each of you should gather supplies in preparation for a great battle. I do not know how long it will be before we are called upon to defend this decision."

After Askuwheteau gave thanks to the Great Spirit for the opportunity to meet together, the people quietly left the long house. As they walked toward their wigwams, their whispers were carried here and there on the wind. No one spoke against Askuwheteau.

Once inside their home, Taipa asked, "What will happen to the Wappingers now, Mother? We are not American. We are not British. Why must we be made to take a side in this fight? The explorers killed some of our people and kidnapped others. The white man's diseases almost destroyed us. Most of our people have already left these lands, and now the few of us who are left are being made to choose sides. Will this be the battle that finishes us?"

Chapter 5

Maggie

Flamborough Head, England

August 1775

Maggie stood on deck watching enormous waves crash over the side of the ship. She tried desperately to hang on, but the water kept coming and coming. Maggie looked up and down the length of the ship for any sign of her family, but she was alone, fighting the massive anger of the storm. Just as another enormous wave was about to crash over her, she awoke with a start.

Tears streamed down her face, and her breath came in quick gasps. Afraid of waking Sean, she forced herself to breathe calmly. Slowly the shadowy forms in the darkness took on the real features of the loft. She looked over and was glad to see that Sean was still sleeping. Maggie lay back down and closed her eyes, hoping that the nightmares would stop. Slowly, sleep returned.

Early the next morning, the crow of the rooster in their neighbor's farmyard awakened Sean and Maggie. Sean hopped up quickly and straightened his pallet. Maggie

lay in bed awhile, trying to catch the wispy fragments of her nightmare.

"You had another bad dream, didn't you?" Sean observed.

"How can you tell?"

"Whenever you stay in bed after the rooster crows, I know you had a nightmare," said Sean. "I like it when you tell them to me. They are not a bit scary in the daylight!"

Maggie laughed. "Oh, but they are scary in the night! This time I dreamt about giant waves crashing over the bow of a ship. There was a huge storm, and I was the only one on the ship. I kept looking for you and Ma and Daud or Ethan and William, but no one else was there."

"I think you are scared about our journey," said Sean. "Daud says it will be very safe."

"I know," Maggie replied. "I try not to worry during the day. But I can't help it if my worries come alive in my dreams at night. Did I wake you up?"

"No," said Sean. "I could just tell. Come on, get up."

"Aye, I'll get up. But let's not tell Ma. She has enough to worry about now without my silly nightmares to worry about, too," said Maggie.

Sean helped Maggie straighten her pallet. They pulled on their clothes over their long underwear and climbed down the ladder. The smell of bread was already coming from the kitchen.

"Ma, you are up very early! Did your worries keep you awake again?"

"Ah, good morning! No, my worries did not keep me awake. The list of all of the things we have to do before

we make our long journey is what kept me awake! I am so afraid that we will not get everything done in time."

"Sean and I will help you, Ma."

"I know you will help me, lassie. Two such good helpers in one house! But sit and have some food first. Then you can both help me with the next batch of bread."

Maggie brought a pot from the hearth and filled two bowls with porridge. She and Sean sat quietly, eating their morning meal. Their heads were full of thoughts and questions about the journey to America.

"When are we leaving, Ma? How many more days?" asked Sean.

Ma laughed. "How many times will you ask me that question? We will leave in two days. Now try to remember that answer so that you will not plague me all day long."

"I'm sorry, Ma. Ever since you told Daud that we were going to go to America with the soldiers, I have wanted to hurry the time along. Is Daud still angry at you?"

"Your father was never upset with me, Sean dear. When he told me that he and Ethan and William must all go to New York City, I knew in my heart that we must go with them. Our family must stay together, even if we must become camp followers."

"What do camp followers do?"

"Oh, Sean, you know the answer to that one, too," said Maggie. "Remember? We will go wherever the British soldiers go. The three of us will live in a tent just like Daud. We will help Ma feed the soldiers. We will have to do their laundry and their sewing, and Ma will nurse the

ones who are hurt or sick. Being a camp follower is a very important job."

"I can't wait until we leave. We are going to sail on a ship all the way to America! Three thousand miles! I wish we were leaving today!" said Sean.

"Sean, how can you leave so easily?" Maggie exclaimed. "I love our home here. I'll miss our neighbors and my friends. I'll miss the trees in our garden and the lovely path to the brook. Most of all, I will miss the cliffs. Do they have cliffs in America, Ma?"

"Well, lassie, I don't know if they have cliffs in America, but I think that what you are really talking about missing is the life that you have here. But if you stayed on here while the rest of us left, you'd be sitting in an empty house with no one to care for. You'll take all of your memories of this place and those cliffs with you, girl. You'll carry them with you in your heart. Whenever you miss this home, just close your eyes and picture it."

Maggie cleared the table and put the dishes on the counter. She began to mix flour, eggs, and milk together. As she stirred, the bits of her dream came back to her. In her mind she saw the violent waves crashing on the deck. With each wave a lick of fear crawled up her back and neck. Her whole family and everything they owned would be on one small ship in the middle of the ocean for several weeks. Her father would come home this evening to help pack for the voyage. Maggie hoped that she would be able to get him alone to share her fears.

Ma mixed and patted the dough, then baked it in large pans. The old wooden shelves by the door were soon

filled with warm, brown loaves. After the noon meal, Ma sent them out to enjoy the sunshine. Leaving their shoes on the grassy bank, they spent the afternoon in the creek building boats of leaves and twigs and setting them asail. Maggie was up to her knees in the water when they heard a familiar voice.

"It's Daud!" Sean exclaimed.

Forgetting their shoes, they ran from the brook across the garden to the front of the house where their father stood with arms wide open. Maggie was finding it hard to run. Her wet skirts kept tangling up in her legs.

"Whose little wet fish are these?" asked Daud.

Sean reached his father first and hugged him so hard he almost knocked his father down. "We're sorry to be so wet, Daud. We were sailing leaf boats in the brook. We made some fine ships, too! Maggie had a dream about a ship."

"Oh, and what was your dream? Not another nightmare, I hope?" asked her father.

"Yes, Daud, and it was an awful nightmare. I was all alone in a big storm in the middle of the sea."

"Now, Maggie, you must listen to me. I would not let you go on a ship if I thought anything would happen to you. The king has a fine navy, and we will travel in one of his big, safe ships. We might run into a storm, but the ship is strong enough to handle the weather. The sailors are very clever, and they will bring us safely to America."

Maggie said, "I know, Daud. I know I shouldn't be afraid, but then the dreams come, and I just can't help it."

"Well, come along now. Let's go in and help your mother. Our plans have changed. We must leave in the morning."

"Tomorrow? Tomorrow? Oh, boy!" said Sean.

—*//*—

Early the next morning, the family set off for the harbor in an old wooden wagon. A neighbor had offered to take them and their luggage to the ship. The horses pulled the heavy wagon slowly. Ma and Daud rode up on the high front bench, and Maggie and Sean were tucked into the back, squeezed between two large trunks. Maggie's stomach lurched with every step.

Finally the horses came to a stop in front of a group of young soldiers. "Can you help us with the load we carry?" Captain MacDuffie called to the soldiers.

One of the soldiers turned around to look at the wagon. He laughed and said, "Well, I think I might be able to help you, Daud."

Captain MacDuffie laughed, too, when he realized it was Ethan. "Where is William?"

The soldier next to Ethan turned around. "Right here!"

The young men carried the family's belongings piece by piece up a long plank walkway and onto the ship. Maggie watched each item leave the wagon, knowing that soon she would have to board the ship as well. Ethan reached up to her. "Stand up now, girl. That's my lassie. I'll lift you down." He swung her out and around, and her feet finally touched the ground. She caught hold of his hand and did not let it go.

The family walked together up the ramp. Captain MacDuffie showed Ma and Sean and Maggie where they would be staying for the journey. The space was small and dark, and many other families were already there. He turned toward Maggie and Sean. "You must promise to listen to your mother. I cannot stay here with you. I must travel with the other soldiers. The officers and I have plans to make, and we will use our time on the ship to do that. When I see you next, I want to hear from your mother that you were well behaved and helpful to her. Remember, the ship is very safe, and before you know it, we will be in America."

"Will we see you and Ethan and William?" Maggie asked.

"I am sure that you will see your brothers from time to time. And I will be sure to check in on you and your mother every chance I get."

Father kissed first Maggie and then Sean, embraced Ma, then turned and left the little room. Maggie's eyes filled with tears, and Sean buried his face in his mother's skirt. She said, "Come now. We must be brave. Time to put our things up and meet all of these other fine people we'll be traveling with these many days."

The ship finally set sail when the sun was directly overhead. The water in the harbor was choppy. The sails caught the wind, which sent the ship bounding through the water. Sean and Maggie stood on deck with their mother, grasping the side rails and waving to people on shore.

The first several days passed quickly. Maggie and Sean met other children and were often allowed to play on

deck. The fresh sea air during the day helped them get through the nights. The small dingy room they shared had quickly become rank with the smells of old food, sweat, and the sickness and waste of so many people. Some were sick from the motion of the ship, others from the dirty drinking water. The women spent most of their time tending to them.

Then, late one night, several days into their journey, Captain MacDuffie came into their room, carrying a small candle to light his way. He had to step over several people until he found his family. Maggie woke from a light sleep to see her father standing over her. She sat up. "What is it, Daud?"

"Shh, girl. Go back to sleep. I've just come to talk with your mother."

Maggie lay back down, but she did not close her eyes. She watched carefully as her father gently shook her mother awake. "You must come," he said. "It's Ethan. He is very ill. So many of the men are. It's the dysentery."

Ma took his hand and held it to her face. Captain MacDuffie helped her up, and the two quietly left the room. Maggie was once again in complete darkness. The blackness hugged the walls of the tiny room and crept up and around her. She felt a scream coming from deep down inside but knew that she could not let it out. Sean was next to her. Even in his sleep, Sean's presence was enough comfort to keep the terror she felt from overwhelming her. Eyes wide open, Maggie waited for the darkness to lift.

Captain MacDuffie took Ma to the soldiers' sleeping area. She could hear the moans of many sick men. They

walked past several cots and hammocks, too many to count. Finally he stopped and motioned toward Ethan, who was lying on a hammock. Ma knelt by his side and put her hand on his forehead.

"He's burning up," she said. The captain brought her a small bucket of water. She ripped a strip of cloth from the bottom of her petticoat and soaked it in the water. Folding it carefully, she placed the wet cloth on Ethan's forehead. He turned to her and tried to speak.

"Shh, Ethan. It's all right now. Mother is here. You try to rest. I won't leave you. I'll stay right here by your side until you are feeling better."

Ethan smiled a small quiet smile. His blue eyes were cloudy and seemed not to look directly at anything. He reached for Ma's hand and squeezed it.

All through the night, Ma and Daud stayed with Ethan. Daud brought more water, and they took turns trying to cool his fever. When the first rays of light filtered into the room, Ethan stirred from his deep sleep and looked at Ma.

"Tell William to be a brave soldier. Tell him I said he must be brave for England—and for you." His eyes slowly closed, and he gave a soft, shallow sigh.

Ma cried, "Ethan? Ethan!" She gathered her son in her arms and pressed his face to her chest. She rocked him back and forth until the captain gently pulled her away.

"He's gone now. Our dear Ethan is gone."

Chapter 6

James

New York City
November 1775

James and his father were hard at work in the print shop. They had just finished setting the type for the weekly edition of *Van Horn's Post* and were about to ink the press when the front door of the shop banged open. A voice called urgently, "Mr. Van Horn! Mr. Van Horn!"

From where he was standing next to the press, James could see into the front room. A man dressed in rough leggings and a warm cloak stood just inside the door. Hanging from a shabby ribbon pinned to his cloak was a medal in the shape of a tree. It was identical to the one his father wore, and James knew that it meant this man belonged to the Sons of Liberty. The man had a burlap bag thrown over his shoulder, and he was brushing a light dusting of snow off his shoulders.

"Da, it's the postrider!" said James.

Mr. Van Horn came out from behind the press and walked into the front room. He held out his hand.

"Clarence, welcome! Are you just in from Philadelphia? Have you news from the Continental Congress for us?"

Clarence pulled off the shoulder bag and shrugged off the heavy cloak. "Yes, Mr. Van Horn. I have news. But I am afraid it is not good news for the Colonies."

"What has happened?"

"Do you remember the petition that was sent to the king? The one they called the Olive Branch Petition?"

Father said, "Of course I remember it. There were several men in the Congress that thought the petition was not strong enough, but they decided to send it anyway. It stated all the Colonies' complaints against the king, but also included sentiments of respect and love for England and for King George."

Clarence said, "Well, Mr. Penn carried the petition across the ocean. When he got to England in August, he tried to meet with King George, but the king would not even see him! He was sent away! The petition was never even read—not by the king or by anyone in Parliament."

"What does our Congress have to say about that?" asked Mr. Van Horn.

"That is the news I have brought for your paper. Congress has just learned that the king has said terrible things about the Colonies. Here, let me read his statement to you." Clarence pulled a piece of rolled parchment from his travel bag. "The king said that 'our Colonies and Plantations in North America, misled by dangerous and designing men, are in a state of rebellion.' King George has given orders to all of his officers and his loyal subjects to stop any rebellion."

"What does it mean, Da?" James asked.

"Wait, James. There is more," Clarence said. "The Colony of New Hampshire asked the Continental Congress to write a constitution for all of the Colonies. The Congress decided they were not yet ready to do that, but they told New Hampshire to go ahead and create their own government."

Again James asked, "But what does it mean, Da?"

Mr. Van Horn took a step closer to James and put his arm gently around his shoulders. "My son, it means that finally the Colonies are beginning to talk about breaking away from our mother country."

"You mean independence, Da?"

"Yes, son, I mean independence."

"I don't think that King George will allow us to be free of England."

"I agree. I don't think he will like the idea at all. We were respectful enough to take our complaints to King George, and he would not even hear them. What other course is there than to rebel? We cannot stay quiet and obedient servants to a king that is not just," said Mr. Van Horn.

"I bet everyone in England is mad at us!" James remarked.

"No, son. Remember, there are many in England who believe we should be free, just as there are many in America who believe we should remain loyal to England."

The postrider walked over to the hearth to warm his hands and feet, and Mr. Van Horn poured him a tall mug of coffee. The two men stood by the fire for a long time,

alternately deep in conversation and at other times staring silently at the flames. James moved the large jug of ink next to the fire to keep it warm. He knew that they would have to set more type before they would be ready to ink the press. This news that Clarence had brought would become their front-page story.

After the postrider had left, James helped his father set type. There was no easy chatter on this day. His father would call for a letter and James would hand it to him. As the afternoon sun slowly left the shop, James used the tinderbox to light lanterns and candles, and then set them about the room. The paper would be very late today, and he would have to hurry his deliveries.

When enough papers were finally printed and stacked, James pulled on his heavy overcoat and warm mitts. He hefted the large bundle of papers and left the shop. This first bunch would go to Mr. Fraunces for his tavern customers. They would be upset that James was late, but their excitement over the news would distract them.

As he walked down Broad Street, James heard the voice of the training sergeant calling to his troops. For many days now, James had slipped away from the print shop to watch from a distance as the militia trained. He stood at a distance watching, often hiding behind a row of trees. He longed to join the men and march alongside the others, hefting a musket of his very own. His father helped the cause of the Colonies by publishing his newspaper. James wanted to help in his own way.

In his hurry to deliver the papers, he allowed himself only a moment to stop and watch. Today, however, the

sergeant spotted him. "Ah, look, men! There is another eager young lad anxious to train with our regiment. This is not the first time I have spied him watching us. How old are you, lad?"

James looked down at his feet and replied softly, "Just 10 years, sir."

The sergeant looked back at his line of soldiers and laughed. "Ten? Come back in four or five years, son. We'll have use of you then."

James hurried away before he could be the butt of more jokes. Four or five years? How could he wait that long? The struggle with England could be over by then! He had to find a way. Father couldn't be the only member of their family to help.

He ran on to the tavern and was in and out before the customers had a chance to complain. The walk back to the print shop took longer because he avoided the militia. He did not wish another conversation with the sergeant. Long into the evening, James delivered papers to various places in the city.

By the time he made his last trips, people were out in the streets talking about the news from Philadelphia. As he neared the corner of Broadway and Wall Street, he could hear the recruiter calling out to the crowd, "Come now, men! Join up against King George! Be the first to put down your name in defense of your country." Colorful pennants snapped in the wind over his head. Three old men sat behind the recruiter, their chance at war long behind them. One played the fife, another the

drum, while the third fired off a musket—its loud thunder bringing shrieks and gasps from the ladies.

Across the street on another corner, a man stood on a platform reading Mr. Van Horn's newspaper article to several men and women who had gathered nearby. When he read about the king refusing to hear the petition, the crowd booed. Another man climbed up onto the platform and yelled, "King George wants to take your money! Do we want that to happen?"

"No!" The crowd roared.

"He wants to put a tax on your tea and your papers and on everything we import. Do we want that to happen?"

"No!"

"When we send a fine man like Mr. Penn to the king with a message, he won't even listen. Is that a fair king?"

"No!"

All around, there was cheering and pushing. Many men were drinking from flasks. Some started throwing bricks through the windows of homes and businesses run by Tories.

James turned away from the crowd and ran toward home, the noise of the crowd ringing in his ears.

When he entered the print shop, his father helped him off with his heavy coat. "Are you all right, boy?" he asked. "The people in the streets have grown restless. I was beginning to worry about your safety."

"Yes, Da. I am fine. Men have been throwing bricks through windows. I don't understand, Father. How will that help? How will destroying things get the king to listen?"

"Well, James, a funny thing sometimes happens when people get caught up in a crowd. Often they leave their common sense behind. The men and women of the Colonies are frustrated with the king. He is so far away, and it takes so long to get word to him or hear any word from Parliament. A letter sent to England can take three or four months to arrive. Sometimes the ship carrying the letter goes down, and the mail is never delivered. All these months of frustration have angered people. When anger is expressed, it can often take a destructive path. Those men and women will not accomplish much by breaking things, it's true. But in being together, they are uniting for a cause. What looks like mayhem to you, a bunch of riffraff causing trouble, is actually the beginning of our journey toward independence."

"What does this mean for the paper, Da? Will you continue to print both sides of the story as you have been, or now will you be able to print your own opinions?"

"I will continue to print the news from both sides, but I will also express my own opinion in the form of a weekly editorial. It will be no surprise to our readers that I am in favor of independence," Mr. Van Horn said. "We can no longer be ruled by a monarchy three thousand miles away. A land as large as ours needs to be run by the people who actually live here. Imagine it, James. You and I will be witnesses to the formation of a new country. We will no longer be Colonies controlled by England—we will become an independent country. Now it is up to the wise men of Congress to determine just what that country will look like."

"I want to help, Da. I am too young to write editorials, and I am too young to train with the militia."

"Listen, James. You are an enormous help to me and to your mum and Hannah every day. I would not be able to print the news without your help. You are doing more than enough, and we are very proud of you. Now it's late. This has been a long and exciting day. Off to bed with you. I'll just tidy up the shop and then I will go to bed as well. Good night, James."

"Good night, Da."

That night as he lay in his bed, James thought about what the sergeant had said. Come back in four or five years! If the Colonies were going to proclaim their independence from England, he was not going to sit around waiting to get older before he could do something to help. There must be some chore or service the militia needed that he could provide.

James lay on his side, softly tapping his fingers on the rough boards of the sleeping loft. Over and over he repeated the same pattern. On nights when he couldn't sleep, the tapping sometimes soothed him. Other nights, it helped him to think more clearly. Tonight the tapping supplied an answer. He finally knew just how to help the Colony of New York. James rolled over onto his back and clasped his hands behind his head. A small smile crossed his face as his eyes slowly closed.

Chapter 7

Joe

Brooklyn Heights, New York
December 1775

Joe lay curled up on his side on the floor of the small tent. No matter how small he made his body, he could not keep out the cold. The one thin blanket he had been issued was no comfort. Frozen rain lashed against the canvas of the tent, and the straw he lay on was soggy from days of storms. He shared the tent, originally built for two, with five other black soldiers who were all at least twice as old as he was. They kindly kept him in the middle of the tent where combined body heat provided the most warmth. But on this harsh night, every man in the tent felt the cold equally.

As the storm raged and the long night wore on, he tried to picture his warm shack at home. His mother would be at the wheel, spinning and singing the evening away. He longed for just a few of the kitchen scraps that she always managed to bring home from the master's kitchen. All he and the other soldiers had had to eat for days on end was salt pork and peas.

The night that he had been taken from his family, he had been given a musket, tomahawk, cartridge box, and powder horn. He remembered how important he had felt when he first held the musket. He had fired a gun before, but he had never owned one. Now the gun stood propped against the tent post alongside the other soldiers' guns. It no longer held any mystery or excitement for him—it was just a piece of cold, heavy metal. The other tools he had been given were crammed inside his knapsack, which now doubled as a hard, lumpy pillow. The whole kit was just something for him to carry during the endless training that stretched from early morning to late afternoon.

He had been living with the soldiers for eight long months. When they first made camp at Brooklyn Heights, the weather was cool, but fair. Summer came, and the soldiers were able to fish and dig for clams and crabs to liven their dinners. Now, in the deep cold of December, the days ran together in a chain of cold and discomfort. They kept their few cannons trained on the harbor, but even the youngest soldiers knew they did not have enough ammunition to win a battle against the well-armed British warships.

During the first few months, Joe was heartsick with loneliness. He spent his spare hours looking out at the wide expanse of water, wondering why he had been taken from his family and home. But as the days passed, he began to turn his homesickness into action, helping the soldiers who had taken sick.

With the first pale streaks of winter sun, Joe pushed aside his blanket. He stood quietly, rolling the blanket up and tying it to his knapsack. There was no need to dress for the day, as he was already wearing every piece of clothing he owned. He stepped over his tent mates and bent low to fit through the small opening.

Immediately the cold wind off the river blasted him, and he tucked his chin far down into his coat. The rain had changed to snow overnight, and the flakes were so thick that he could barely make out the huge dirt mound that the soldiers used for ovens. Already several soldiers were tending the fires. Cold had brought an early end to their night's sleep as well.

The circular mound of dirt stretched ten feet across. Large holes had been dug into the side of the mound about every two feet. Directly above and behind these makeshift hearths, bayonets had been pushed into the mound and then pulled out, leaving holes that created a draft for the fires that were built in the hearths. All the cooking for the regiment was done here. Joe smelled salt pork, but he remembered corn bread and porridge, bacon and sausage.

"Mornin', Joe," said one of the men near the ovens.

"Mornin'."

"You goin' to the sick again today?"

"Yes, sir, I am," Joe said. "It isn't doin' anybody any good for me to lay in that tent and be freezin' when I can tend the sick and be freezin'."

"Your mama would be proud of you, boy."

"My mama would be tendin' the sick if she was here. I'm just doin' what she would do," said Joe. "Besides, some of them boys haven't got anybody. It isn't right to be near dyin' with nobody you know sittin' with you."

Joe reached into his knapsack and pulled out a battered tin bowl. He filled it with a sticky clump of porridge that he scraped out of the bottom of one of the pots set to keep warm above the ovens. As he shoveled a spoonful of the bland lumpy mixture into his mouth, he thought of hot biscuits and butter.

"Look at that boy smile! He eats that slop and he smiles. How do you do that, boy?"

Joe said, "I'm eatin' what you're eatin', but I'm thinkin' of home. That makes all the difference."

Joe finished the porridge. He wiped out his bowl with some wet sand and put it back into his sack. He left the warmth of the ovens and walked toward the row of tents that had been set up for the sick. When the soldiers first arrived in April, there had been only one such tent. Now the line of tents numbered seven, each filled with men sick with the fever, dysentery, or smallpox.

Joe went into the first tent and walked close to each man. He greeted the men if they were awake, asking if he could get them anything. He brought water to a few. As he walked by one of the men, a hand reached out and stopped him. Joe looked down at a face so covered by oozing blisters that he immediately looked away.

"Oh, now, boy, don't turn away," said the soldier. "I know I look bad, but you make me feel worse when you turn away like that."

"I'm sorry, sir. What can I do for you today?" asked Joe.

"Can you write?"

"Yes, sir," said Joe. "I can write."

"How do you know how to write, boy?"

"My master, Master Michael, he taught me my letters. Nobody is supposed to know that though. I'm not supposed to know how."

"Well, I won't tell. I haven't got anybody to tell. I need you to write a letter for me, boy. Can you take down what I say and put it in the mailbag for me?"

"Yes, sir," said Joe. "I can do that. I have to go and find paper and somethin' to write with, and then I'll be back to do that for you."

"I thank you. You best hurry, boy."

Joe touched the man's hand and hurried from the tent. The snow swirled around him, and the wind sent his coattails flying. Pulling the brim of his felt hat further down onto his forehead, he leaned into the wind and headed for the officers' tent. Once inside, he stood quietly, waiting for an officer to notice him. Two men sat at a table, reviewing maps and making notes.

After several minutes one of the men looked up and said, "What is it, boy?"

"Please, sir, is there paper and ink to spare? One of the men in the infirmary is dyin'. He wants to send a letter to his family."

"There is precious little paper," the officer snapped. "We must conserve it for maps and documents. I can't spare even a small amount for such a task."

Joe did not answer the man but simply turned to leave the tent. As he did, the officer stood up and spoke quietly. "Just a minute, son. Here you come on the wishes of the dying, and I can't even be bothered to find you a piece of paper. Wait there. I will find something. This interminable waiting wears on all of us."

Joe waited. In just a few minutes, the officer brought him paper, a small bottle of ink, and a feather quill. Thanking the officer, Joe promised to return what he did not use.

Once back in the infirmary, Joe found a small canvas stool. He unfolded it and sat down next to the man whose skin was littered with smallpox blisters. His eyes were closed, and Joe gently nudged his shoulder.

"I'm back, sir. What can I write for you?" asked Joe.

"Thank you. This is a kind deed you do for me. This letter needs to go to the post office in Providence, Rhode Island. My wife will find it there."

"What all do you want to tell your wife, sir?"

The soldier thought for a minute. He cleared his throat and then spoke haltingly.

Dear Rebecca,

My dearest wife, I hope this letter finds you in good health. It comes to you in a strange hand, as a kind young boy has volunteered to write it for me. This winter is unusually cold and harsh. I fear for you and the children. Have you been able to see to the livestock? Is there enough

feed for them to last until spring? If you need to sell any of the animals to provide for the children and yourself, you know that I trust in your decisions. This cruel struggle keeps me from being able to take care of those I love best.

I send a message that will be difficult for you to hear. I am ill with smallpox and do not expect to live more than another day or two. Already it has become difficult to breathe. I feel my lungs beginning to fail as I tire with the effort of going on. My greatest sadness is in knowing that I shall never see you or the children again.

You have brought me great happiness and I know that I leave the children in your good care. Should you ever have need of anything, call on John Williams. He is a good friend and neighbor. I know he will do whatever he can for you. Give the children my blessings and remind them to always be honest and hard-working.

My dearest wife, I want you to know that as I leave this world, my last thoughts are of you and our family.

All my love, Your devoted husband,
Samuel

As Joe finished writing the last words of the letter, Samuel touched his sleeve. "What is your name, boy?"

"I'm Joe, sir."

"Thank you, Joe. I am most grateful for your kindness."

Joe sat next to the soldier for several more minutes, watching as he lapsed into a restless sleep. He tucked the letter into his own shirt pocket and left the infirmary. After returning the pen and ink to the officers' tent, Joe put Samuel's letter in the mailbag. He walked across the icy rocks and stood at the edge of the cold East River. Joe thought about the path the letter would take, how it would sadden a woman so far away from this cruel shore. He imagined her opening the letter—happy to be receiving news from her husband, only to be crushed by the news of his early death.

Joe thought about King George. Was he sitting in his fancy castle? What fine foods was he eating? Did he know that Samuel would soon be dead? Did he know how miserable the soldiers were? The river kept lapping at the shore, wave after wave of cold, dark water.

Chapter 8

Taipa

Lower Hudson River Valley, New York
January 1776

Taipa sat on her sleeping platform, warmly wrapped in animal skins. A brutal winter wind lashed against the side of the fort, making it hard to hear the other members of her family. At her feet a ball of twine grew as she slowly pulled apart plant fibers and twisted them into a string. Her hands were stiff from the cold, and the string making was slow work. She knew that if she kept her hands busy, the slow tempo of winter might be made to move along a bit faster.

She turned toward her mother. "It is so hard to wait for Nixkamich to return."

"There is no way for us to know how long he will be gone," her mother replied. This storm will make his journey a long one. We cannot tell how many days he will stay in New York City or how many days it will take to travel back home."

"I wish he didn't have to go during the moons of snow. I wish he was home here with us so I would know that he was safe and warm."

"Taipa, we must have news about the soldiers. Now that our nation will side with the Americans, we need information about their plans. Your grandfather hopes to meet with General Washington. But Washington is an important and busy man, and it may not be possible to see him right away."

Taipa turned back to her work, picking up a long section of dogbane. First, she pulled the outside casing off the plant, and then she began to pull apart the thin, tan fibers. When she had three good pieces of fiber, she held them together with one hand and rolled the other ends against her thigh, spinning the fibers into a string. The twine would be used to reinforce their wigwam when it was once again warm enough to move back to their summer home.

Mother sat just across from Taipa, and her hands were also busy. Carefully, using a complicated series of knots, Mother was making a strong band from plant fiber. This tumpline would be used to hold a cradleboard firmly to her back. When the snows were finally over and the earth began to warm, there would be a new baby brother or sister for Taipa. Mother and daughter would take turns carrying and tending the infant as they moved through each new day.

The cool gray light of the winter sun slowly faded. The light of the campfire was not enough for her handwork, and Taipa set it aside. She wrapped herself in a thick

bearskin and walked across the fort to sit with her cousins.

"Taipa, have you seen the storyteller yet?" asked her youngest cousin.

"No, I have not seen him. But even with the storm, I know he will come. He carries his stories proudly and would not want us to wait with empty ears and hearts. What story will you ask him for?"

"Will I be the one to choose?" Taipa's cousin asked.

"Yes! Nixkamich told me that you will be the one to choose the story. Which one is your favorite?"

"I love the stories about the stars. I will choose the one about the seven dancing sister stars."

"I love that story, too," Taipa said. "The storyteller will be glad to tell that story for you and for all of us who wait for the moons of snow to finish."

The many families who lived inside the winter fort spent the evening talking and singing. Taipa's eyes were just closing when she heard muffled voices raised in greeting. She looked up to see a tall man being welcomed by the men and women of her nation. After removing many layers of animal skins, he listened carefully to words whispered by Taipa's mother and then walked directly toward her sleeping platform.

"I am told that someone here has earned the honor of choosing this night's story. Who is this honorable person?"

Taipa's cousin said, "Nixkamich says that I am to choose the story."

"Ah, and what have you chosen?"

"I would like to hear the story of the seven dancing sister stars."

"That is a good choice. I will tell the story."

The storyteller sat down on one of the many sleeping platforms. Children came from all over the fort to sit at his feet. The grownups sat behind the children and on the sleeping platforms. Slowly the rustling of movement stopped, and everyone leaned toward the storyteller. In a deep voice, he began.

"Long, long ago, a man from this village walked to the great river to fish. Even though his mind was focused on the job of catching fish, he was able to be grateful for all of the wonders that met his eyes. He saw Grandmother Sun ready to slip below the horizon. He heard birdsong in the trees and watched insects buzz around the many flowers along his path. The hard-packed dirt of the path still felt warm to his bare feet.

"When he reached the riverbank, he stopped to uncoil his fishing line. The gentle breeze from the river brushed across his face, bringing a new song to his ears. He looked up and down the shore of the river but could not see anyone. But when he looked up, he saw a beautiful basket floating down from the sky. He was so afraid that he dropped his fishing line, ran into the woods, and hid behind a large elm tree.

"The basket landed gently on the edge of the river, and seven girls climbed out. Each was dressed in a beautiful long white gown and slippers. Ribbons of pale pink and blue trailed from their shiny black hair. Their song floated in the air, more beautiful than the great river and

all of the trees and flowers that lined its shores. The girls joined hands in a circle and began to dance to their own song.

"The man's eyes were filled with their beauty. Forgetting his fear, he, too, began to sing. When the girls heard this strange, deep voice coming from the trees, they screamed and ran toward the basket. As quickly as they could, they jumped in and were whisked back up into the darkening sky.

"The man was sorry that he had frightened the beautiful dancers. He thought to himself, 'I will come back to the river when Grandmother Sun once again begins to sink into the horizon.'

"The next day he returned to the river to listen for the song and watch for the basket. This time when it arrived, he stayed hidden and watched the girls sing and dance. After they had danced together in a circle, each girl took a turn dancing alone. Watching the last girl dance, the man thought his heart would burst from her beauty. He left his place of hiding to be closer. The girls heard his footsteps, and once again ran to the basket to escape.

"The man ran toward the basket but was not able to catch hold of it. He dropped to his knees on the riverbank, his eyes full of tears. 'Wait!' he called. 'I just want to talk to you! Please, don't leave!' But the basket floated up, up, and out of sight. The man forced himself to walk home, his slow steps leaving scuff marks in the dirt.

"Once again he returned to the riverbank. This time he stayed hidden, listening and watching as the seven

beautiful girls danced and sang. He heard their laughter—like tiny bells in the wind. Just as they were climbing back into the basket, he ran from his place of hiding and grabbed hold of the last girl, the most beautiful of all. She screamed for her sisters to save her. 'Help! Let me go! Let me go!' But he would not release her, and the basket left the riverbank with all of the other girls calling to her and crying her name.

"'Why have you stolen me? I belong with my sisters in our sky basket,' she cried.

"The man said, 'Please, I do not mean to scare you. My heart is full of love for you. I would like you to stay here and be my wife.'

"'Oh, I cannot live here,' she said. 'Our father is the Sun and our mother is the Moon. I am part of the Pleiades, a cluster of seven stars. I must go to my home in the sky.'

"'Then I will go with you! I will live in your Sky World,' he replied.

"'My father will not allow it. You must let me go!'

"The man said, 'Let me come with you just this one time. I will speak with your father. If he orders me away, I will not come to you again.'

"The young girl agreed to his plan. They waited all night and day for the basket to return. Her six sisters made room in the basket, and they were lifted up beyond the clouds into the Sky World.

"When Father Sun heard how the man had fallen in love with his daughter, he said, 'I will let you live here in the Sky World, but from now on, you will all live far away.

You will live so far away from Earth that you will never be able to dance there again.'

"The man said, 'Father Sun, if you allow my wife and me to visit Earth, you have my word and hers that we will always return. In that way I can show her the beauty of Mother Earth as she will show me the beauty of the Sky World.'

"Father Sun thought for a long time. Finally he said, 'You and your wife may visit Earth. I believe that you will return. As for my other daughters, they will not be allowed to leave the Sky World. They will choose their husbands from the stars around us.'

"So the man and the beautiful dancing girl were married and lived forever with her six sisters in the Sky World, low on the horizon in a bright cluster of stars. When the man and his wife visit Mother Earth, only six stars are seen in the constellation of Pleiades."

When the story was over, the people were silent. Each one considered the beauty of the story and the lesson it offered. Slowly the grown ones brought gifts of food and tobacco to the storyteller. As the last gifts were put forth, the door at the end of the fort opened, and Taipa's grandfather stepped in. He turned quickly to close the door against the frigid winds.

Taipa ran up to him and cried, "Nixkamich, you are home! I am so glad that your journey is over."

"I am glad to be home!" said her grandfather.

Mother called to him, "What news do you bring us from the city by the big water?"

"Soldiers fill the city. On one side of the river are the soldiers from across the sea. On the other side of the

river are their brothers. They lie in wait, practicing firing their guns and walking up and down in straight lines. There is much shouting. But there is also great hunger and sickness among the men. If the fight is not settled soon, there may be no one left to stand at battle."

"What are the soldiers saying? Does anyone know what the plan is?"

"At night the streets are full of angry people. It seems to me that the man who speaks the loudest is the man that people listen to. A gang will gather, and there is much shouting. Sometimes they break windows in the houses and businesses. They pull the taxmen out of their homes and cover them in tar and feathers. They parade these poor souls up and down the streets on the back of a wagon. People come from all over the city to throw rotten fruit and coarse names at the men.

"The last night that I was in the city, a crowd of men and women walked through the streets. They chanted verses full of hate for King George of England. Some of the men were dragging a figure made of cloth. When they got to the center of town, they hung the figure by its neck. It represented their lieutenant governor, who did not support the Colonists when they protested the Stamp Act. I cannot understand how these men, who call themselves Sons of Liberty, can believe in their hearts that this is the way to win freedom."

"Will we still fight with the Americans?" Taipa asked.

"Yes, Taipa. This fight troubles me greatly. I do not want our people to be a part of it. But we have given our word. We will stand with the Americans."

Chapter 9

Maggie

Staten Island, New York

February 1776

Maggie stood over yet another pot of watery soup. The steam from the boiling soup had sent the shorter hairs around her face into springy curls that now framed her tired expression. Every few minutes she looked up at the night sky, hoping to see the first rays of sunlight, willing it to bring warmth to her icy hands and feet.

A long line of red-coated British soldiers wound away from Maggie's pot. In turn, each man stood before her, holding out a small bowl to be filled with the morning meal. Her actions were automatic—she had long since given up greeting or even looking at the men who waited in her line. Her shoulders ached from stooping over the pot, and her apron was crusty with drippings from the soup ladle. Trails of tears and soot from the heavy cook-fire smoke wound their ragged way down her cheeks.

She longed for the familiar sounds of her home. At this time of day, her father would just be leaving the house to

milk the cow. Her mother would be waking her, shooing her out from under her warm bed covers to feed the chickens and to look for eggs. After morning chores she would have enjoyed a large breakfast—eggs with rashers or sausage and fried potatoes.

She would have spent the morning helping her mother spin and weave cloth for new summer clothing. In the evening, Daud would have played his fiddle, and Ma would have read from the family Bible. But this was not England, not home. When her father and brothers had been ordered to sail to New York City, her mother had bundled Maggie and Sean up with their sparse belongings, and they had followed their father to this new world of America. For weeks now, ever since leaving the ship, Maggie had been helping her mother cook for and serve the hundreds of soldiers stationed on Staten Island under the command of the British General Sir William Howe.

The men trained hard. They stood in the rain, snow, and sleet, steeling their shoulders against the unrelenting wind. How the men were able to face each new day was a mystery to Maggie. There were reports of battles in other Colonies and there were always rumors of coming battles, but it seemed that nothing ever happened in the Colony of New York. While the men trained endlessly for a war that never seemed to come, Maggie and her mother and brother stayed in the camp, cooking meals and doing laundry and sewing for the soldiers.

She looked away from her work just long enough to check on her mother. She, too, stood over a pot, serving

bowls of watery soup to hungry, impatient men. Her mother's movements were mechanical, the spoon going back and forth from pot to bowl in a series of short, choppy motions. Since Ethan's death, Maggie's mother had lost her cheerful spirit. She rarely spoke. Often Maggie had to call her name several times before her mother would respond.

"Girl, mind who you're servin', will ya?" grumbled a soldier.

"Sorry, sir. My mind wandered is all," said Maggie.

The soldier's face gentled into a small smile, and he said, "Aye, are ye thinkin' of fair England, lass?"

"Aye, sir. And how my family used to be before all this."

"You mustn't think of it as being gone, but think on how it will all be like that again, lass. One day we'll all go home," said the soldier.

"Yes, sir. One day," said Maggie. But Ethan would never see England again, and they would never be the family they once were. She filled the soldier's bowl with soup.

Finally the long lines faded away, leaving the women and children to scrub the pots and spoons from the morning meal. There would be long hours of sewing and laundry and more cooking before the evening meal of salt pork and peas was served.

As she tipped the last pot upside down to dry, Sean ran up, yelling and waving a paper. "News! I've brought a newspaper! Maggie, read it to me!"

"Sean, where have you been?" his mother exclaimed. "How many times have I told you not to wander away? I need you here to help with the work, and I can't keep

track of you and serve the soldiers at the same time." All the excitement drained from Sean's face. Mother pulled him close and said, "Ah, sorry, my special boy. My tongue seems to lash out cruel words before my brain has time to think about it. Give Maggie the paper, boy. We're grateful indeed for any bit of news."

Several women stopped their chores. Pulling their long cloaks tighter against the wind, they crowded around to listen. Sean wriggled out of Mother's hug while Maggie scrambled up on top of a large upturned pot so that more might be able to hear.

"One of the soldiers brought this paper across the water from New York City," Sean said. "He said it was important."

In a loud, clear voice, Maggie said, "It's called *Van Horn's Post*. It says here that a man named Thomas Paine has written a book called *Common Sense*. In it he calls for all of the Colonies to declare independence from Britain. Mr. Paine says that 'the custom of all courts is against us, and will be so, until, by an independence, we take rank with other nations.' Then he says, 'Nothing can settle our affairs so expe...expe...'"

Mother looked over Maggie's shoulder. "Expeditiously. That means speedy and efficient at the same time."

Maggie read, "Nothing can settle our affairs so expeditiously as an open and determined declaration for independence."

"Independence!" Several women in the crowd repeated the word.

"And it also says that the Colony of New Hampshire has written its own constitution calling itself a State, not a Colony! The editor of this paper, Mr. Van Horn, is calling on the other Colonies to join in and write their own state constitutions."

Maggie looked at her mother. "What does it mean, Mother? Why is everyone talking about independence? What will happen now?"

Mother helped Maggie down from her perch. "I think it means that the war will come to New York soon. I think it will be a long war, and that many more men will be hurt. It's a fearsome decision to be made. Will the Americans sacrifice their safety to fight a war for independence? Will the British sacrifice the safety of their soldiers to try and continue to control the Americans?"

"What's the answer, Mother?" asked Maggie softly.

"I don't know, dear. I truly do not know."

Chapter 10

James

New York City
April 1776

Mrs. Van Horn lifted Hannah from her cradle and held the baby gently against her shoulder. "Let's just go see what has happened to your brother, shall we? He should have been home hours ago." Opening the door into the print shop, she walked through it and into the pressroom. Carefully holding the baby's frock away from the ink-stained counters and shelves, she walked to the front of the shop.

"James?" Mum called. "James!"

Appearing from behind a fully loaded bookshelf, Mr. Van Horn said, "James isn't here. He left with the last stack of papers to be delivered a long time ago. I assumed that he was at home with you by now. He is not in the house?"

"No, he never came in. Where in the world can that boy be? Have you noticed that he is coming home later and later in the afternoons? Now it's near time for supper and no sign of him. The streets aren't safe with all of the

soldiers milling about. Dear, I think you should go and look for him."

Mr. Van Horn untied his apron and hung it from a hook on the wall. He crossed the room to his wife and laid his hand gently on her cheek. "We mustn't worry," he said. "I'm sure he has just run into some friends and forgotten the time. The days are warmer and the afternoon light lasts a bit longer. I'll go and have a look. It will do me good to get some fresh air." He kissed the top of Hannah's head and turned toward the door. "I'll have him home in no time."

He left the shop, stepping down the wooden stairs and onto the thick boards set in the heavy spring mud that was Broad Street. As he walked, he looked in the windows of the shops that lined the street, hoping to find his son lost in thought, watching one of the hard-working artisans. From time to time, he stopped an acquaintance and asked, "Have you seen James?" Each one shook his head.

As he neared the green, he could just hear the voice of the drill sergeant hollering orders at the militia and the faint sounds of a drummer keeping time for the soldiers. He barely glanced at the men, so familiar was he with the presence of soldiers in his city. He continued looking into shop windows and inquiring about James.

Mr. Van Horn crossed the street and began to make his way back toward home, checking the shops on the other side. The men in the militia now formed one long line. Each man held his musket upright against his right

shoulder. A small drummer boy at the end of the line tapped a steady beat, keeping the soldiers in step.

Suddenly Mr. Van Horn stopped. He stood in the middle of the boardwalk while other townspeople passed him by. Something about the drummer boy had caught his attention. Slowly he turned around and walked back toward the militia. There, at the end of the line of soldiers, was James, carefully beating time on his drum.

Mr. Van Horn ran across the street. He grabbed James roughly by the shoulders and whirled him around, lifting his feet right off the ground. "What is the meaning of this?" he demanded. "What are you doing here?"

Before James had a chance to speak, one of the other soldiers grabbed Mr. Van Horn and pulled him away from James. "Hey, Mister, no one bothers our drummer boy! Move on now and leave him alone!"

"I will not move on!" shouted Mr. Van Horn, pushing the soldier away. "This boy is my son, and he does not have my permission to be here! Kindly take your hands off me, sir!"

The soldier looked first at the father and then at the son. He took just a small step away, ready to come to the defense of the boy if needed. James stood with his head down, still tightly holding his drumsticks.

"I'm sorry, Da. I know that I have deceived you by not telling you about training with the militia. But I want to help my country. I am too young to be a soldier, but I know how to drum. I asked the sergeant if he needed me, and he said yes. So, here I am.

"Look, Da!" said James. He lifted his head to look his father in the eye. "I really am helping. The drum is used to give signals to the soldiers. Once the guns start firing, they can't hear the sergeant anymore. He tells me what to say, and I use the drum to say it. The soldiers can hear the drum—even with all of the muskets firing. It's very important, Da. Please say you'll let me do it. I promise I won't be hurt. I'm sure the British wouldn't shoot a young boy. Please say yes."

Mr. Van Horn pulled James close. "My dear son. I do not give you enough credit. Your ears have heard all the words that have been flung about by the fine men who visit my print shop. I fight the tyranny of the king with the words in my paper. These good men may have to fight the king's soldiers with their muskets and their bayonets. The men of New Hampshire and South Carolina have had the courage to write their own state constitutions. Any one of us could be charged with treason, but still we continue with our actions because we know in our hearts that we are right.

"Each man must follow his heart in this difficult time. Those of us who have felt the freedom of living without the harsh rule of a king are not willing to return to that control. We are ready to sacrifice for that freedom. How can I deny my son the same privilege? I am very proud of you, James. Your ability to drum may save many lives for this militia."

Mr. Van Horn leaned down to look directly into James's eyes. Very quietly he said, "Now, about your

mother. I do not think it would be wise to mention this to her, do you?"

"No, sir," said James. "She wouldn't understand."

"Fine, then, on this issue we agree. This shall remain a secret between men. I will tell her that I found you and gave you permission to stay with your—well, let's call them friends, shall we?—a little longer. You are to be home within the hour, understood? Your mother will be holding your dinner for you. And you are not to be late to dinner again. You must make an arrangement with the sergeant so that your mother's wishes may be honored."

"Yes, sir. Within the hour."

He gave James a small pat and then stepped away. He nodded at the soldier who had come to the boy's defense. Walking away, he heard the sergeant say, "Ready, boys? And hut, two, three, four. Hut, two, three, four." With each number he heard the sharp beat of the drum.

⸻

It was almost an hour later when James began the journey home. He walked swiftly—he was hungry, and he had made a deal he was determined to keep. But as he turned the corner onto Broadway, James encountered an unruly crowd of Colonists and was caught up in their determined march down Broadway. One man, who seemed to be their leader, called out in anger.

"Shall we send King George a message?"

"Yes! Yes! Send him a message!"

"Just down Broadway in Bowling Green is a grand statue of King George riding his beloved horse. I helped

to put that statue up, but now I say, let's take it down! Down with King George!"

Many of the people in the crowd repeated what the speaker had said. "Down with King George! Down with King George!"

"Ladies and gentlemen, follow me!"

The entire crowd started to move in the direction of the statue. James was swept along in the enormous tide of people. As they neared Bowling Green, the crowd grew even louder. One man tied a lasso knot in the end of a heavy rope. He spun the rope over his head and then let it go, spinning it out toward the statue. The rope dropped down around the head of King George, and the crowd cheered as the rope was pulled tight around the statue's neck. Several men used their walking sticks to push up under the statue's pedestal. More men put their weight into pulling on the rope, and soon the statue was toppled. An enormous cheer went up from the crowd.

James heard one man say, "Aye! 'Tis a good sign. The lead in that statue can be made into musket balls, a far better use for it, if you ask me."

James watched in amazement. What good could this do? Surely the king would now be madder than ever. He ducked through the crowd and hurried home to the safety of his family, wondering how much longer that feeling of safety could last.

Chapter 11

Joe

Brooklyn Heights, New York
July 9, 1776

Whenever Joe's shoulder muscles screamed so loudly that he thought he could not lift the shovel one more time, he let his mind drift back to his mama's kitchen. Softly he sang the words of one of her spirituals, and somehow he was able to go on. The men had been digging for several weeks. It was back in April, when the snow first began to melt, that the camp had stirred with excitement.

"What is it? What is happenin'?" Joe had asked one of the older men in his tent.

"Why, boy, General Washington is coming here. He knows he has to protect New York City. Those British may soon be sailing their warships right up the river."

"General Washington is comin' here?"

"Yes, boy, that's what I am telling you. Look sharp now."

Later that same day, Joe and all of the other soldiers stood in long formation, row after row of soldiers. General Washington rode past the men. He sat tall in the saddle, his dark blue uniform in contrast to the pale April

sky. When he reached the middle of the lines of troops, he reined in his horse and turned to face the men.

"Gentlemen, I know that your rations are short, your blankets are thin, and the cold winds of winter have plagued you. I am going to ask even more of you now. We must fortify this area against attack. All of you will be involved in this work. You must dig the trenches deep and build the walls high. Those walls must be well-packed. The British may have more soldiers, more ships, and more guns than we do, but they will never have more heart or determination. I will not ask any man to do more than I will do to win our freedom. I ask this in the name of our country—America!"

He turned his horse once more and rode on past the remainder of the troops. Joe had watched the general out of the corner of his eye until he was out of sight. The one word that stayed in Joe's mind was *freedom*. Did Washington mean that Joe, too, would be free? Or did the freedom that they would fight for belong only to the white soldiers?

That word, *freedom*, still pulsed within him three months later as he spent yet another day digging trenches. Now the hot summer sun beat down on them. Most of the men were bare-chested, and sweat rolled down the sides of their faces. When they first started fortifying this place called Brooklyn Heights, the men thought the work would last just a few days. But the British were slow to make decisions, and the threatened attack never came. So, they dug. There were long days of

mud and sun with too little food and too little water. Even the hymns of home were scant comfort.

Joe heard hoof beats and looked up to see a rider approaching the fortification. The man barely stopped the horse before he swung out of the saddle and ran up to the commanding officer.

"Sir, I have news from Philadelphia! General Washington has ordered that this be read to all of your soldiers at once!"

The officer called for the drummer. He gave orders, and the young boy signaled the troops to form ranks. Slowly the men pulled themselves from the trenches, glad for any reason to lay down their shovels. When all the men were gathered, the officer climbed atop a storage chest to be more easily seen and heard.

"General Washington sends word from headquarters. Congress has declared independence from England! Richard Henry Lee wrote a resolution stating that the Colonies ought to be free and independent States. The Congress voted to support that resolution. Thomas Jefferson has written a Declaration of Independence. Representatives from the Colonies have signed the Declaration, and I am instructed to read it to you."

"Sir!" said one of the junior officers. "Did the representatives from New York sign the Declaration?"

The officer scanned the document. "No, sir. Their directions from the legislature were unclear. The New York Provincial Convention will meet in White Plains this evening. I assure you that they will vote with the other Colonies in support of independence. After they vote,

the New York representatives will sign the Declaration. From this time forward, these Colonies will be known as United States. Gentlemen, I will now read to you from the Declaration of Independence."

The officer then read the entire document, as well as a long list of grievances committed by King George III of England.

"Gentlemen, this declaration was signed by the members of Congress. You now serve in the army of the United States of America!"

Throngs of soldiers cheered and whistled. Hats were thrown, muskets were fired into the sky, and grown men cried and hugged each other. When finally the officer could once again get the attention of the men, he said, "Three cheers for the United States of America!"

The lines of men responded, "Huzzah! Huzzah! Huzzah!"

Joe walked slowly toward the trench he had been digging, the words *freedom* and *independence* still ringing in his ears. As he bent to pick up his shovel, he heard a familiar voice call, "Joe! Joe! Over here!"

Before he could even turn toward the voice, a look of sheer joy crossed his face—the same look that had always met that voice. Strong hands pulled the shovel from him, and he was lifted off the ground in a huge bear hug.

"Master Michael, whatever are you doin' here? If your papa finds out, he'll be some kind of mad!"

"Joe, don't you see my uniform? I've joined up! I couldn't let you fight in my place. What kind of man would send a young boy to do his duty for him? It took

me awhile to do the right thing, but I knew I couldn't live with myself if I didn't do my part to keep my country free of that tyrant in England. Sometimes my father is an unreasonable tyrant, too! I've been looking for you for months. Are you well, Joe? Your mama sends her love."

"Is she all right? Are they all doin' well, Michael?"

"Yes, Joe. Your mama and papa are doing just fine. They are a lot happier knowing that I am going to be sending you home to them. Come on, now. Let's go and get your things, Joe. We need to get you home."

Joe looked around. The cheering continued. Shovels were strewn all over the rocks, abandoned in celebration of their new country. He looked at Michael. "No, sir, Master Michael. I'm glad to see you and to know that Mama and Papa are well. But I am not leavin' here, no, sir. This is my fight, too. These boys here, well, I'm one of them. I am not leavin' my boys to go home to my mama. What kind of man would do that, Master Michael? No kind of man that I want to be."

Michael started to argue. "Now, Joe, you need to... ." But he stopped when he realized that the determination of Joe's words matched the look in his eyes. He held out his hand. "Then we'll fight together, Joe. We'll watch our nation's birth together."

Joe shook Michael's hand and said, "Come on, Master Michael. Let's get you a shovel!"

Chapter 12

Taipa

Lower Hudson River Valley, New York
July 1776

Taipa and her grandfather sat on the ground near their wigwam. Grandmother Sun warmed their backs as they bent toward the clay pots in their laps. Taipa watched Nixkamich closely and copied the movements of his hands. Few were left in their nation who worked with clay, and she wanted to learn from his skill and talent. Most of their people preferred the iron pots that the European traders brought to their village. Only a few women clung to the old ways and still cooked in the clay pots of their past.

Few words passed between the two. Their hands smoothed the clay, gently rounding each pot's rim. Grandfather held his in both hands, his thumbs moving in slow circles over the surface of the clay, as he turned it round and round.

Mother walked quickly toward them. Bound firmly to her back, a small baby boy lay quietly in his cradleboard. "Father," she said. "There is news. General Washington sends word that the Grand Council of the Colonies has

declared independence from England. These strong words will be followed by war. You must leave us now."

Grandfather handed his unfinished pot to Taipa. He laid his rough hands on either side of her face and tipped it up toward him. "Your eyes watch carefully so that your mind learns. You will carry many of our lost traditions on to the new ones who will be born to our nation. My heart swells with pride when I look upon my granddaughter."

He stood up and faced his daughter. "Yes, it is time. Go and tell the people to prepare. We will all leave with the next sunrise. You must take the children and all of the other women and go to the fort. There are provisions there, and you will be safe. When it is time, we will come for you, and our people will once again live peacefully on this land by the great river. We will spend this day making ready for our journey. When the sun rises again, we will go our separate ways. Our warriors must fulfill our promise to the Americans."

Tears filled Taipa's eyes. She tried to blink them away, but they overflowed and fled down her cheeks, dripping onto the pots that she held in her lap. She lowered her head, ashamed to show fear in front of her grandfather. She knew that he would see the water stains on the pots and that he would scold her for her childishness. She waited for the harsh words, but instead she felt his hands on her face once again, this time brushing away the tears.

"Be strong, little one," he said. "Be strong for your mother and for your small baby brother. Reach down inside yourself and find the strength of all those who came before you. Face this new challenge with a heart full of blessings and a mind full of knowledge. I know we will return to this place and find all of our people healthy and content."

Taipa put her hands over her grandfather's hard-calloused fingers. She felt their strength and their warmth before he pulled away and headed off to gather the other men of their nation. Two more tears splashed down onto the pots, but Taipa willed that those would be the last. She stood and carried the pots inside the wigwam. She would bring them with her to the fort to finish. They would be a good gift for her grandfather upon his return from the battle. Taipa wondered how many days or even seasons it would be before she could offer him her gift.

Early the next morning, the women stood silently together and watched the men of their nation load supplies onto a small framework of branches. Two of the men tied strong rope between the wooden sleigh and one of the horses. When the last of the warriors had mounted his horse, the group turned as one and rode out of the village. There were no last words or goodbyes. All of the people had shared those words during their last night together.

Grandfather led. When they reached the narrow path that wound close to the riverbank, they rode in single file. The sun slowly worked its way across the sky, and still the men rode on. From time to time, they would stop and let the horses drink from the river. The men ate cornmeal and syrup from small leather bags that hung from their belts. They did not want to take the time from the journey to build a fire and cook.

The sky was streaked with the final reds and oranges of sunset when the men reached the soldiers' encampment. They dismounted and waited while Nixkamich walked into the camp area and asked one of the guards if he could see the commanding officer. He was led to a large canvas tent and told to go inside.

Several candles placed on a small map table and on storage chests provided light inside the tent. Seated at the table was a man in full military uniform. His long black hair was pulled sharply away from his face into a neat ponytail. Thick spectacles rested on his nose just above a thick dark beard that covered most of his face. When he heard grandfather's step, he stood and said, "Welcome!" He walked toward Nixkamich and said, "I am General John Sullivan. I was in hopes that you would arrive today. Thank you for coming. We are in a most dangerous position. General Washington has told me that we are far outnumbered by the British soldiers. If we have any hope of winning this battle, we must have information soon. Will you and a few of your men be able to sneak across the water under cover of darkness? You will use one of our canoes. Any information that you can bring to me will be of great service to this effort."

"Yes, we can do that. We will go across the water and tell you what we see," said Nixkamich.

"Thank you. Your people will not be forgotten for supporting America in this struggle," said General Sullivan.

"General, our people have been forgotten many times before. Your promise, although well-meant, is empty to us. This great struggle will take place on land that was

hunted and lived on by our people for many seasons before the white man came with the guns and alcohol and diseases that took the lives of so many. You speak of this country as if it belongs to you. Do you not remember that there were people already living here when your ships came from Europe? If I traveled now to Europe, could I stand on the shores of England or France and claim the land as my own?"

The general could barely look Nixkamich in the eye. "No," he said. "No one would let you claim those lands."

"Our nation, the Wappinger Nation, believe that we are born free, answering only to the Great Spirit. White men seem to become slaves to other men they call king. This is not something we understand. We do believe that it will be easier to trade with the Colonies if they become one unit instead of thirteen different nations. We must continue to watch over the land that is our home. For these reasons we will support you in your fight with England. We are ready to begin."

"I'll have some of my men take you to the canoe."

Nixkamich followed the soldiers across a rocky beach to the edge of the harbor. He listened carefully as the men pointed out across the water. Then he and two other men quietly slipped into the canoe, soundlessly dipping their oars into water as black as the night that closed in around them.

Chapter 13
Maggie

Staten Island, New York

August 22, 1776

It was just past midnight when Maggie woke, surprised to hear her father's voice in their small tent. She rolled over and looked across her sleeping brother toward its source. Light from a candle in her father's hand pierced the heavy black of the moonless night. She waited for her eyes to adjust to the night shadows. She could just make out the outline of her father sitting on the ground next to her mother's pallet. He held her hand in his, his face very close to hers.

"William has already landed on Long Island with General Howe, the British commander. I have been ordered to sail with General Cornwallis across the Narrows to Gravesend. I know that you had hoped William and I would be together to watch over each other, but that is not to be. He is a wonderful soldier and very well trained. You must gather all of your strength and courage now, and take care of Maggie and Sean.

Keep them close to you this day. You may hear gunfire and cannons, and you must be brave. I will come back to you, my dear, and your William will return to you as well. Now I must take my leave."

Mother did not answer. She brought her husband's hand to her cheek and held it there. Maggie did not speak to him, did not tell him that she was awake. She couldn't think of a thing to say. Father stood, looked quickly in the direction of Maggie and Sean, and then, stooping, left the tent. Without the candle the tent was once again cloaked in black. Maggie heard her mother settling back on her pallet. From her soft sniffles, Maggie knew that she was crying.

As soon as her father left, Maggie wished that she had spoken. She wished that she had cried and yelled and begged him not to board the ship. But she knew her father would have left, no matter how much fuss she made. Wonderful Ethan had left them. Would her father leave them, too? Tears squeezed from behind her closed eyelids and slid down her face. She was glad her father had not stayed to see her tears.

All through the long hours before dawn, Maggie waited for sleep to find her again, but it would not come. She kept seeing her father's tall silhouette leaving the tent. She wondered where William was and what he was doing. Was he still asleep? Would he fire his gun at someone today? Would the Americans fire at her father and William? Who would survive this battle? Could her mother lose another son and still go on?

Dawn finally came. "Maggie! Sean! Time to get up! We have breakfast to cook and men to serve," Ma called. She smiled at both of them and left the tent. Sean scrambled up out of his blanket and pulled on his trousers. He reached for the apron that hung from a peg on one of the wooden tent posts.

"Maggie, get up! You usually have to chase me out of bed. Are you sick? What keeps you in bed after Ma's call?"

Maggie knew the answer. Her feet would not move; her body would not behave. Her mother had tried to use the same voice to wake them that she used every day. She had fooled Sean. But she had not fooled Maggie. What she heard in her mother's voice was the same thing that kept her from leaving her pallet. It was fear.

Fear had walked into the tent with her father and flung itself at them. Fear had stayed behind after her father had left.

Chapter 14

James

Brooklyn Heights, New York
August 27, 1776

It was nearly dawn. James had been camping on the northern slope of Brooklyn Heights with his militia unit ever since the end of June. During his first week, a lookout for the Americans had reported sighting dozens of British warships. When General Washington heard that these ships had arrived in New York Harbor, he ordered half of his troops to Brooklyn to prepare for battle. James would not let himself think of his mother or her tears on the day when he announced General Washington's orders at the dinner table. Thoughts of his family tore at his heart and sapped his strength.

He loosened the top button of his jacket, hoping to ease the rash that grew ever wider on his neck and chest. The sun had been down for several hours, and still the sweat ran down inside his shirt. Thick clouds of black flies were an endless irritation. At night their constant buzz kept him awake. During the day they riddled his skin with bites and stings. Dirt and sand lodged between his

stockings and shoes and rubbed the skin off his heels. This miserable itching and chafing were not what he had dreamed of when he became a drummer.

The flies had awakened him again this night, and he left the tent, hoping it might be cooler outdoors. He sat alone, looking out across the water, wishing himself home. When his father and the men who read the papers in Fraunces Tavern had talked about independence, it sounded important and necessary. Their words had stirred him, and he followed his heart to this cruel place.

A man on horseback rode up to the long line of tents. He climbed down from his horse and walked from tent to tent, leaning in to tell his news to each group of soldiers. James left the water's edge and walked back toward his own tent in time to hear the messenger say, "Colonel Edward Hand has been keeping watch on the British from an outpost near their camp. He sent word that five days ago, the British crossed the Narrows from Staten Island and landed thousands of men and 40 cannons. Their troops have now breached our line at Jamaica Pass and mean to attack! Prepare yourselves, men."

James watched the man continue on his slow journey until he faded into the shadows. Inside James's tent men were checking their muskets. One loaded his gun by wrapping a small piece of greased cloth around a heavy lead ball. He pushed the wad down the barrel of the musket. James knew that the tighter the fit, the more firepower the gun would have.

Having no musket, James slid his thin wooden drumsticks into his belt and cinched it a little tighter around his waist. All around him, men prepared for battle.

Chapter 15

Joe

Brooklyn Heights, New York
August 27, 1776

Joe lay on his stomach in a shallow trench. Flies swarmed around his feet, biting his ankles. Men on either side of him swatted at them, but no matter how much shooing they did, the flies came right back. Joe had given up trying to swat them away. It just made him feel hotter.

The first soft lines of pink streaked the horizon. "Dawn," thought Joe. "Mama will be startin' the morning meal now. Papa will already be in the fields, checkin' those fences."

Just behind the trench, an officer walked back and forth. He drew his saber and held it high. "Be steady, men. Hold your fire until you hear my order. We need to make every musket ball count. It won't be long now. As soon as there is enough light, the British will attack."

Joe kept his finger on the trigger of his musket. Every few minutes he lowered his head and looked through the sight on his gun. He had killed before. He had killed squirrels and deer and brought meat back to his family.

He tried to imagine aiming his gun at a man, tried to imagine squeezing the trigger.

He dropped his head, resting his forehead on the cool soil. It was quiet in the trench. Each man was focused on his own musket, deep within his own thoughts of home. A man dropped down into the trench and lay down next to him.

"Mornin', Joe."

"Master Michael, you can't be here! This is the slave regiment! There are no white men in this trench."

"There is now," said Michael.

"You have to get out now! You go on back to your own regiment, Michael! You have no place here. You can't be watchin' over me anymore. I'll be fine, Michael, I'll be just fine."

"And what place do you have in fighting a war for liberty? Are you a free man now, Joe? Have you and your family ever been free? Will this war make you a free man?" Joe did not answer.

"Think about it, Joe," Michael said. "White people came to this land from Europe. Some came to make money, like my father. Some came to practice their own religion without fear of persecution. Others came to be missionaries to the Indians. They wanted to show the Indians how to live life the "right" way—their way.

"Your family didn't choose to come here. They were torn away from their own family and their own land, and they were brought here in chains against their will. They were sold at auction to the highest bidder like a cow or a horse. Now white men want to be free from what they say

is the tyranny of King George. Look up and down this trench and see who it is we are making fight our war for us. Do you think the rich men who sent these boys to fight in their places will care—will even notice—if these slaves die in battle?"

Joe looked at the long line of dark faces, all armed and ready to fight against an enemy not their own. His hand moved to his chest, gently fingering the scar left by Lord Underhill's branding iron.

"I'm staying with you, Joe. We'll fight this war for America's liberty, and then we'll fight another war for your liberty. You have my word on that, Joe."

Michael adjusted the barrel of his musket, propping it on the bank of mud in front of him. He moved just a little closer to Joe, looked through the sight, and put his finger on the trigger.

Chapter 16

Taipa

Lower Hudson River Valley, New York
August 27, 1776

Grandfather sat near the campfire with the other men from his nation. He could hear the gentle whinnying of the horses nearby. Soft ocean breezes played with the fire, throwing shocks of light onto the painted faces of the men. Soon the sun would rise. Grandfather reached into the bag tied to his belt and threw a pinch of tobacco on the fire.

"Great Spirit, we ask that you watch over us as we go into battle this day. We know that we are outnumbered three to one. The British have hired hundreds of Hessian soldiers to help them in their fight against America. We have seen their ships and their weapons. The enemy has more men and more guns. We will fight hard, and we will know that you are watching. We are grateful for your many gifts.

"It has been very hard to decide what to do. We go into a battle that we do not understand. It is a battle of brother against brother. These men think that they own

the land and the water and the animals. Our people know that it is the Creator who must be answered to. One day we hope the white man will understand this."

"Nixkamich," said one of the warriors. "Speak the words of Benjamin Franklin and Canassatego. Their wisdom will warm our hearts."

"Benjamin Franklin is a wise man. He is a great listener. He has learned of our ways and finds them strong and good. Benjamin Franklin once sat at a council fire with Canassatego, a man from the Onondaga Nation."

"What did the great leader Canassatego tell him?"

"Canassatego told of the forefathers who established a union and friendship between the six nations of the Iroquois. He told of the League of Nations that became powerful and respected by neighboring nations. Finally, Canassatego told Benjamin Franklin that if the Colonies would form a league, they, too, would be strong and powerful."

"What should we do now, Nixkamich?"

"We will help the Americans join together in a strong and powerful league. Come, the light is changing, growing stronger. It is time to put out this small fire and start a much bigger one."

Chapter 17

The Battle of Long Island

August 27, 1776

Maggie sat by the creek, her toes in the cool water. She leaned over and scooped the water up in her hands, splashing it onto her face and neck. Sean stood in the middle of the creek, sending small leaf boats into the current.

"Maggie! Sean! Come and help gather firewood for the cook fire," called Mother.

Sean turned to Maggie. "Why do we need to worry about cooking today? The soldiers all left."

Maggie stood up and let her petticoat and skirt fall back into place. "Come, Sean. Mother must think they will be back soon."

James stood at attention next to the captain of his regiment, a drumstick in each hand. Behind James stood row after row of soldiers, each armed with a musket and bayonet. The men were all from different regiments and different states. There was no one uniform, just a clashing sea of colors and fabrics—

blue wool, buckskin, bare chests, homespun coats with patched elbows and missing buttons. The men stood silently, listening for a signal.

―――※―――

Mother held the baby while Taipa served soup to many of the women in the fort. As she spooned the soup into the wooden bowls, she looked at the strong, safe walls of her winter home and wondered where her grandfather was. Pictures of him injured or ill flooded her mind, and her hands started to shake. Sensing her distress, one of the older women took the soup pot from her, and Taipa ran to the comfort of her mother's arms.

―――※―――

Michael and Joe lay in the trench as waves of British soldiers advanced. The early morning light reflected off bayonet blades and buckles. When the first soldiers were so close that Joe could see the fear on their faces, the officer behind him yelled, "Fire!"

James repeated the officer's order on his drum. All across Brooklyn, muskets exploded, sparks spit up into the sky, and lead balls flew. Through the smoke and the noise, the soldiers could still hear James beat out the order over and over on his drum.

"Fire!"

"Fire!"

"Fire!"

Afterword

On August 22, 1776, approximately 20,000 British troops landed on Long Island from Staten Island. Under the command of General William Howe, brother of Admiral Howe, they began their march into combat on August 26, ultimately marching through the unguarded Jamaica Pass and circling around behind the Patriot soldiers. The Americans, under the command of General George Washington, were completely outnumbered. On August 27, they were attacked from three directions by British and Hessian troops. Some were trapped and slaughtered. Others fled and ended up cornered at Brooklyn Heights, the East River behind them. Then, for some reason, General Howe (against the advice of another British general) chose to wait rather than keep up the chase.

For two days, in heavy rain, both Patriots and British hunkered down in their trenches. Washington watched from a redoubt at Brooklyn Heights, not sleeping for 48 hours. Realizing the strength of the British forces and sensing that victory was impossible, he decided to retreat just after midnight on August 29. In a daring move, protected by dense fog, Washington silently evacuated about 9,500 troops—all that remained of the Continental Army—across the East River to Manhattan in a motley flotilla of small boats that he had commandeered. The British never caught on until it was too late.

In the few hours of fighting that was the Battle of Long Island, over 300 Americans were killed. About 1,400 were wounded, captured, or missing. Total British losses were about 60 dead and about 300 wounded or missing.